BENEATH THE AURORA MOUNTAINS

BOOK 1 IN THE
WINGS OF ALCHEMY
SERIES

TORI EINHER

Edits by BB Garin

Cover Design by Tori Einher

Cover Illustration by Artist of Realms

Chapter Illustrations by Jeanie Estheria

For those like Dori—

The ones who give when they have nothing left
Who carry the weight so others can rest
Who are hurt in silence and heal in shadows
Who trade their peace for someone else's calm.

This story is yours. I see you.

Believe in the power within you,
May you find your wings and the strength to soar

CONTENT WARNING

This story contains depictions and discussions of trauma; including PTSD, abuse (emotional, physical, and/or psychological), death, violence, and chronic illness. These themes may be distressing or triggering for some readers. Discretion is advised.

This book is not intended to provide professional advice or therapeutic guidance. It represents the author's personal journey and perspective, and is not a definitive account of any condition or experience.

The intention of sharing this story is not to cause harm or discomfort, but to raise awareness of these issues as well as encourage healing for those who struggle with/have struggled with these topics.

ZALOR
SAPPHIRE FALLS
XANTOS HEARTH
ZALOR HIGH
SAPPHIRE FALLS

N
W
E
S
Elandvor
Whispering Forest
Adenike Concourse
Teresi House
Sielu Villa
Lithos Ridge

N
W
E
S
BITTER
BREW BOX
DRAGON
LOUNGE
SIRENS
COVE

DELMIRA ISLAND
MOUNT SERAPHINA
CANO VALLEY
KAIROS' CRAG

Welcome to Delmira Island

Whispers of legends suggest that Delmira Island once served as a portal to a concealed realm, where a mystical city of fae slumbers beneath the veiled mountains. Eons past, and now the Aurora Mountains cloak the city, veiling it from mortal eyes. However, magic from the city still flows through the island, which is why the aurora borealis shines in the sky above all year long. This wonder of the world lead the island to become a big tourist destination; people would travel from all over to see the gorgeous colors dance in the night sky. The entirety of the island played on the theme of the supernatural to entertain the tourists. Shops selling fairy pendants or witch spell books, gothic cafés for the vampire-loving customers, and restaurants with enchanting food and drink. The tourists reveled in the myths and mysteries. If only they knew how true the stories were...

ℂHAPTER 1

The clouds had been lingering on for what felt like an eternity, but today the sun finally peeked out and the island felt more like home again. It felt more like home than Endora's actual house. The heavy rains had finally calmed after a raging summer, and left the grass lush and warm. A cool breeze hit the hills so perfectly the world seemed a little more peaceful. With the ocean roaring below her feet, the tranquil mountains behind her, and the beaches with all the people miles away, this was Endora's favorite spot on the island. She tried to enjoy the tranquility despite her bitterness of the chaos at home this morning.

"Selfish maniac," Endora hissed under her breath as she grit her teeth in frustration. Tears threatened to claw their way to the surface as she pictured the flames that engulfed her door barely an hour ago. "4 AM," Endora said, speaking into the open air above the cliffs.

Her frustrations at her older brother waking her up that morning clouded her peace. Another ridiculous screaming fest for absolutely no reason. "Like how are you so angry at 4 AM?" she exclaimed to herself shaking her hands in front of her. She exhaled violently and shook her head to try and lose the visual. Endora reminded herself that a year from now she'd be moving away to college, not that she knew where she was going yet. Nevertheless, senior year started in just a couple weeks, she just needed to survive that and then she would be out of that house.

The sun had just begun to creep over the distant horizon so it didn't help charge her powers much. Not that this area received much sunshine during the day, but the lack of people allowed her mind to rest from constantly perceiving emotions all day. That and the fact it was outside the fae realm and far away from home made it the perfect space for her. Though no amount of distance could keep the haunting thoughts away for long. She breathed easy for a while allowing her mind to turn off, until the memories flooded her. The visual of the flames this morning ignited an old memory she could never shake. It's like she was frozen in time as the flashback took over her, not even being able to hear the ocean below her.

A simple day sitting at her desk sewing together the first top she ever made. Sitting back from her tiny corner desk wedged between the wall and her bed in her little room, she closed her eyes and wiggled with glee. As she placed it on her body she smiled. She was so proud of herself, it may have taken 17 attempts, but she finally did it! A beautiful velvet fall-orange top, tight to her chest but flowing in waterfall-like ruffles down to her navel and hips coming longer in the back. She twirled in admiration of her newest creation.

Then she heard the yelling.

She took a deep breath. Another moment of joy robbed from her. She stood tall and opened up her bedroom door to step into the line of fire once again.

"No," Endora shook her head to block the rest of the memory from entering. "Today will be a better day," she said to herself as she sat up taller, closing her eyes. She touched the grass around her and focused on the sound of the waves crashing against the rocks at the base of the cliff she was perched on.

Today would indeed be different. What she didn't know is it would change her life forever.

Endora ran her hands through her long blonde hair, starting at the top of either side of her head and pulled her fingers through the purple tips at the base of her thick waves. She breathed in the air, slightly salty from the ocean breeze but also deeply fresh from the mountain herbs and plant-life at her back. She heard someone coming and turned to the right. She swiveled her head as she saw a girl that appeared to be her age headed in her direction; she sensed her magic but also sensed darkness, odd for a fairy who's magic was light and life. She stared, head cocked to the side.

Her long black hair cascaded effortlessly down her back, swaying in the breeze with each step she took. With long legs and prominent cheekbones, she was tall and slender, radiating beauty. A twinge of jealousy struck Endora; she wished she could be that beautiful.

Lost in her own thoughts, suddenly the girl was standing before her.

"Hi." Endora said sitting with her hands on her propped up knees.

"Hi," the girl said, stepping back, "Forgive me, I didn't realize anyone was up here and just kept walking," she said looking at her feet.

"Oh no worries. I'm Dori. Are you here on vacation?"

"Me? Oh no I live here." The girl was thrown a bit by her friendliness but it added to the probability of her being a fairy.

"Oh. I haven't seen you before. Are you new to town?" Dori said, looking at her.

The girl laughed to herself. "No my family has been here a while. We just keep to ourselves for the most part." Feeling as if she had let slip too much, the girl began to turn away. Though she was reluctant to leave the peaceful scene and her new acquaintance. She was curious to know more about this bright girl.

Dori sensed a glimmer of inquiry in the girl. "You don't have to go." She patted the grass beside her. "There's plenty of room. I like to come here to avoid people and listen to the waves."

The girl smiled turning back. "Me too," she said as she took a seat a few feet away.

"Sorry if I stole your alone time. I'm here a bit earlier than I usually come," Dori said shyly.

"No. It's okay." She wasn't sure that was true but there was something peaceful about the other girl's presence that made her say it anyway.

Dori sat there quietly turning back to the ocean to give the girl some of the silence she probably came here for.

"I'm Mae, well, Andromeda. But I go by Mae," the other girl offered.

"Nice to meet you, Mae." Dori turned her face towards her and offered a smile.

Mae wasn't sure she should fill the air with any more talk but for whatever reason she felt herself relax, yet was feeling too fidgety to sit in silence when the other girl had been so friendly. "So are you escaping crazy family drama too or just don't like all the vacationers?" Mae teased lightheartedly.

Dori rotated her entire body toward Mae, hopeful of a new friendship beginning to kindle. "A little of both," she disclosed smiling, feeling like a little kid sharing toys.

Mae also turned. "I figured. You mentioned you come up here often, and I do the same thing," she said honestly. "It's just so peaceful and quiet."

"It's been a daily thing recently," Dori chuckled.

"Part of living in a beach town I guess." Mae relaxed on her arms behind her, looking toward the waves again.

"Yeah, you'd think we'd be used to it," Dori put her feet out in front of her and leaned back on her hands as well, "but it's always best to avoid it during peak season."

"Your family or the vacationers?" Mae taunted.

Dori laughed. "Well, I'm here year 'round if that gives you any clue," Dori responded. She smiled and laid flat in the grass looking up at the sky. "Do you live on the north side of the island? I don't often go up that way, that might be why I haven't seen you." Dori realized that was probably a stupid question since Mae walked up the hill from her right not left where the North beaches were.

Mae couldn't admit to living on the east without giving away too much detail. "Yep." She quickly responded, "I like to walk along the cliffs toward the volcano and was on my way back when I saw you." Mae nodded as she noted *"Good thinking"* to herself.

"Gotcha. I'm from the south part, and go to the west for the markets. And then come here in the mornings but have only really been to the north for events. Oooooh, like the annual Solstice bash!" Dori elated. "Or the Harvest Festival that's coming up?" She asked as she sat up in excitement.

Mae felt a little awkward. She sat up, sitting a bit hunched, and admitted shyly, "I haven't actually been to either of those," pausing briefly, "like I said, we mostly stick to ourselves." She looked down a moment then realized she had been to an event there before. "I have been to a New Year's Party there before though."

"Oh, the festivals are amazing! Such good food and the decorations are so fun! You should really try and make it this year." Dori pressed.

Mae smiled. *"It would be nice,"* she thought.

Ding Ding

Dori's phone buzzed in her pocket. "Sorry" she offered as she sat up more and pulled it out to check.

NEW MESSAGE FROM ABIGOR

STOPPED BY YOUR HOUSE BUT YOU WEREN'T HOME. MEET ME FOR BREAKFAST?

Dori sighed. "I have to go," she sighed, standing up from the ground.

"Alright," Mae exhaled, giving a wry smile.

Dori turned to walk away but wanted more; forsaking her bashful tendencies she turned back and said, "I don't mean to be forward but would you maybe want to get together again?"

Mae was startled but had enjoyed this brief interaction with this girl more than any socialization in as long as she could remember. "How about tonight? Meet at the Dragon Lounge in the West around eight?"

"Sounds fun," Dori smiled. "See you there."

Dori truly felt like today would be a better day. She practically skipped through the forest to the portal. She spun quickly, bolting into the air, shrinking to the size of a doll. A shiny mystic fog surrounding her as she did so, with sparks of light shining all around. Her wings emerged from the middle of her spine outward, shiny in the daylight that had just crested over the base of the mountain that lay before her. Her wings shimmered like stained glass, glowing yellow and orange with a faint purple outline. Her now small body glowed yellow and she inhaled deeply, feeling revitalized by the uplifting social exchange. She flew through the invisible portal and looked up into the glistening fae realm, Meltembra.

Taking to the sky, Dori flew over the city toward the concourse in front of the beaming castle at the center of the island. Zalor was the metropolis of the realm, where fairies of all types lived in harmony. Well, in a perfect world it would be truly harmonious, but like any civilization they made mistakes and had struggles. Zalor was the center of the fairy world, at its center was Elandvor, the city's castle, containing a tower with a portal to every major city in Meltembra. The fae realm was very similar to the human world, laid out nearly identical, but civilization looked different here. For one very obvious reason, magic lived free here. The fairies were free to be themselves here, never forced to hide and able to use their magic openly.

At least, most fairies were. Dori didn't feel so free in most of Zalor any more. If she wasn't home, she was out in public where everyone knew her, or assumed they knew her, and would ask questions about a wedding that she hadn't even begun planning yet.

The land declared her betrothed, but Abigor hadn't even proposed yet. Which she was grateful for because she couldn't bring herself to say no, no matter how much she wanted to be allowed to decide her own path in life. The city felt the Einwhai had brought them together, and their match would help unite the factions again. Many regions across Meltembra were divided by fairy factions, some even going as far as closing their borders to other factions. The divide created a weakness in the connection to the Einwhai, if not corrected it would continue to deplete their magic. The council had done much in the last few decades to create a sense of unity and fight against the divide. With Dori's legacy in the council and Abigor being from a dominion of Night

Fairies, their union would push the unity of the different regions across Meltembra.

Shadowhead was a dominion near the equator, where a large sect of Night Fairies lived to keep watch over the population of witches and lost fae there. It was one of the only places on earth where the witches followed the fairy guidelines of magic. Abigor was born in Shadowhead, and had lived there most of his life before moving to Zalor. Abigor and his younger brothers had all shown promise in their Night fairy talents from an early age. Being the oldest, this led to an invitation being extended to Abigor to attend the prestigious Zalor high. The school boasted a renowned Night Warriors Training Corps, NWTC for short, and had offered Abigor and his family a generous stipend to help with the move and cost of the house. His single mother was exceptionally grateful, so they accepted the opportunity. Dori met him the following year when she began high school. They quickly found out that their younger brothers were in the same year and already friends. The two families molded together quickly and Dori loved how welcoming Abigor's mom was to her. Dori was the daughter she never had. Abigor's standing with the Night fairies made him a suitable match for a young fairy anticipated to join the council, quite the "power couple" as many referred to them.

Everyone thought they were destined to be the next generation's "power couple". In the beginning of their relationship Dori really felt that they were. Abigor used to be the perfect boyfriend, sweet, handsome, and thoughtful. Even if she didn't believe it herself, Dori was stunning. Abigor saw that from the moment they met and his adoration of her had lifted her spirits and seemed to save her from a low spot in the beginning of high school. He had given her a safe space away from home, she knew he would protect her, physically at least, no one could protect her from all the emotional damage she faced at home. But at least he brought her out of some of the emotional pain she faced in the halls at school.

She flitted back to human size to enter the café. Most of the city operated in human size, it had been that way long before the great divide as the city was once open to humans. Some of the city had since updated to function in fairy form, but Adenike Concourse, that lead to the main bridge of Elandvor, the ancient castle, would never alter in that matter. Most every building in the concourse was over a thousand years old, built with ancient stone and carved arches. Though the castle was open to the public it was still heavily guarded, and many sections of Elandvor were not open to just anyone, like the tower at its center. Long ago the tower was a public place where any fairy could use the Faebana, the portal junction that laid at the top of the tower to different parts of the realm. It was a safe haven where fae of all kin could come and bring their requests to the royal family. Now just below the Faebana sat the offices of the council and you had to have priority clearance to use the portals.

Dori saw Abigor sitting in the back of the café, as soon as she walked through the door he stood up, his tall, bronze physique becoming more obvious as he towered over the tables next to him. Dori glided through the crowded tables to meet him, no one noticing her but naturally a couple girls at a table near Abigor couldn't take their eyes off him. Café Fortress was right outside the entrance to the bridge, so it was the busiest spot in the city especially in the mornings. Most every table on the main floor was filled, Dori looked towards the upper floor of sprite-sized tables, even more packed than the tables below. Dori smiled thinking about when she and Blythe went to the Café that mirrored this one in the human world, with little glowing figures to mimic the fairies here. Young fairies often went to add to the 'illusion' of the fairy patrons, bringing magic to life for the tourists that couldn't get enough of the lore of Delmira Island.

"Hey Babe," Abigor said touching Dori's arm and giving her a peck on the cheek.

They sat across from one another, the waiter approaching with their coffees.

"Wow, such service," Dori said smiling up at Sprig, the short blue-haired barista that Dori had known since she was in middle school.

"Abigor put your order in so it'd be ready when you got here," Sprig said.

"Well, I do know your favorite drink," Abigor boasted. Which Dori let him believe, luckily since she was a regular here Sprig actually did know the drinks she liked and replaced Abigor's order every time. The young fairy was only a few years older than Dori, she had really admired him since he moved to Zalor. He left his family of Dryads in the rain forest to come to Zalor High and study Water magic. It was practically unheard of, which is why Dori admired his determination so much. She remembered how much he was criticized in his first years here, but he persevered and now was one of the strongest young Water fairies around.

"Thank you," Dori said as she raised the mug to her lips.

Sprig placed a plate of sparkling pale blue macarons down.

"New flavors to test out. On the house," Sprig said smiling as he turned and walked back to counter. Dori gave him a thankful smile

Abigor glared past his girlfriend at the boy behind the counter. "What was that about?" He said turning his attention to Dori.

Dori looked at him a little startled, "What do you mean?"

"The free food? And the look he gave you?" Abigor asserted.

"You know I review food and beverages here, and I've known Sprig forever, he's a friend," Dori defended.

Abigor side-eyed the tables nearest them. "We will talk more about this later."

Dori exhaled and sipped her coffee.

"Did you go to the North beach again this morning?" Abigor asked.

Of course that's where she always said she was, no one knew about her favorite spot. Well, not until this morning.

"Of course. I left a little earlier than usual, after the night we had," Dori answered with exhaustion straining her voice.

"Yeah, your brother alluded to something when I stopped by this morning."

Dori tried to hold back but let out a scoff.

"I know he can be difficult, but give him a break, the other Sun fairies have been giving him a hard time." Abigor added.

"You know first hand what he does, why are you defending him?"

"I'm not. I just know how difficult things have been lately and maybe if you cut him some slack. Yah know, use those Meta fairy powers of yours and have some empathy. Maybe things would lighten," Abigor said trying not to sound mocking.

It didn't work. Dori chewed on her cheek just thinking how much of a joke this was, her side ached with the pain of her anxieties.

"Let's just talk about something else." Dori was angry enough to care less if taking a macaron made her boyfriend upset. She grabbed the teal one sitting back in her chair in defiance, and it felt good.

Abigor looked at the teal cookie in her hand and then back up at her.

"Fine," he asserted. Then he continued on about the latest mission and how much fun he was having training new recruits.

Being a talented young Night fairy, Abigor was plucked from the masses to be in the ranks of warriors in Zalor, protecting the city. Since graduating just over a year ago, he was still in the beginning of his climb to working with the great council, and spent his days training recruits. At first, Dori encouraged his pursuit of working with the highest ranking warriors, but it wasn't long before she felt him slipping into the same postulated attitude as the pompous Night fairies who hunted dark creatures for sport.

"I'm excited to be heading back to Takidaisu, though I wish we were going back in spring when the cherry blossoms are in bloom, it's unlike anywhere else in the world," Abigor said about his upcoming mission. "But the Water fairies over there support the lost fae and witch-creatures like family, there is even talk of opening the barriers to welcome them into Meltembra!"

"Would that be so bad?"

"Dori, we've gone over this," Abigor said dismissively. "I know you want to see the best in people but the lost fae are *lost* for a reason. Night fairies understand that, I don't understand why Meta is so willing to ignore that." Dori hated being grouped with the opinions of her faction, especially since she hadn't even declared her faction yet. Meta were the ones with the dimensional magic and were responsible for the barrier after all. But because of their friendly and welcoming nature they were seen as the pushover faction. "Anyways, we have to go over and work with the sect of Water fairies to help with a Selkie issue, I can't really go into too much detail. But there's Fauna over there encouraging the

Water district to embrace the Selkie and welcome them to the land," Abigor continued shaking his head at the thought.

Well, Fauna are the fairies of life. Dori wanted to say but avoided the confrontation. She enjoyed her snack and took some photos of the different colored macarons to post a review later, mostly ignoring her boyfriend in front of her. She spent so long being interested in his stories, and that interest used to be genuine. But the more he got involved with the Night fairies the colder he was to her, she looked him in the eyes and longed for the days when she first fell for him. She recalled the laughs they shared and how sweet he used to be. He still was at times, but the laughs and tenderness were scattered throughout their life now. She allowed her smile to remain though, for his sake, and cherished the memories.

CHAPTER 2

Mae sat for a few more minutes pondering the interaction. She had sensed something in the girl on the hill she hadn't sensed so strongly before—light. She must be a fairy, but it was rather odd the aura she sensed on her. She could sense...darkness. She wasn't a witch, that much was clear, but never had she chanced upon one who bore the essence of both light and shadow. But as the sun beams were rising up the cliffs she readied to leave. She loved to play this game. Waiting until the final second, she sprang up and headed towards the volcano. She halted at the base, sheltered from the sun's rays by the ashy clouds above. She waited there a moment, but knew she had to walk around and get back to Cano Valley, the only place on the island that remained safe from the sun all day long. Apparently, the volcano on the island surfaced with dark magic nearly a thousand years ago and ever since then the dark clouds and ash remained floating at the crest. However, the magic of the Aurora Mountains held so much power that the volcano's darkness wouldn't dare travel into the island, so the deep clouds formed a shelf above the valley below on the east side of the island, blocking any traces of sunlight. This was the reason why many vampires made their haven on the eastern shores of the island.

She hugged the volcano, walking slow, taking her time getting home. Not like she had much choice. There were some tunnels that led to the towns on other parts of the island but most of the storefronts let the sunshine in all day long. Another downside of living on an island. Plus most of the time those tunnels were festering with arrogant Night fairies ready to pick off any vampires trying to sneak their way through the island.

Home it is. Their village was small but it was the only place in the world her people didn't have to hide their identities and could walk outside during the day without turning into roasted marshmallows. Well, at least the only place she knew of.

Walking past all the "Forbidden", "No Trespassing", and "DANGER KEEP OUT" signs, Mae let out a sigh. As far as many islanders and any tourists knew the volcano was active, even though it had been dormant for centuries, so they stayed away from the valley just below it. She had lived here so long she'd gotten used to the seclusion, but she had always dreamed of more. After meeting someone new this morning, someone that treated her like a person, for the first time she felt like she could actually have more than this secluded life.

Mae prolonged her time outside the valley best she could and decided to wander up. The volcano wasn't very steep so she simply just walked the incline upward. Kicking dusty reddish grey pebbles between her feet, killing as much time as she could. If she stayed in the right spot she could go up pretty high, avoiding the sun rising in the east. She ascended far enough to admire the thick orange and red veins on the volcano. It gave the appearance that the volcano was active and was convincing enough that humans rarely went anywhere near the east of the island. The theory is that when the volcano sprang from the earth it was stained with dark magic, forever tainted by the witches who brought it to life. Serving as a warning to all those approaching the valley of the darkness that awaited them, and stood as a reminder that, just like the volcano, the Seraphina would forever be tainted in darkness.

Tracing her fingers along the crystalized colors in the stone, Mae gazed upon the mesmerizing deepness of the colors. The orange, brighter than fire itself, and the red so dark and vibrant someone could tell her it was actually blood and she would believe them. It would make sense for the reminder of the Seraphina's curse to be calcified in blood, given how much was spilt that day. Mae's eyes peeked over toward the ridge just beyond the valley, the first sign of light beyond the vast cascade of shadows. The tall stones upon it looked lifeless compared to the sparkling ocean beyond the ridge.

One dark coven believed that after the separation of the realms the ridge would hold immense power as it was where the fairies gathered to create the mirror island. The Seraphina, malicious and merciless, their quest for power knew no bounds; for the longevity of life and the strengths of their greatest enemies, Night fairies, eluded them. Thus, they sought to draw upon the magic of the ridge, to harness the enchantments of the fae realm. But it all went horribly wrong.

The very fabric of reality trembled, and the volcano appeared from the earth below, quivering and igniting sparks from its bellows; for their quest for power had summoned forth a tempest of chaos. Darkness shot from the crest of the stones in Lithos ridge, a dark cloud as black as night covered the valley, a poisoned magic enveloped the witches, their curdling screams were heard around the island. One by one they fell to the ground silent and lifeless. They awoke new creatures. Creating what we know today as vampires.

Mae's family had come centuries later. Her father had been a supernatural archeologist, and became obsessed with the Seraphina and the legends of Kairos' Crag. His intelligence and arrogance made him the perfect right hand for the pretentious dictator ruling over Cano Valley back then, Zagan. So they never left.

Mae didn't quite understand why he was even still in power, he ruled with fear and had no mercy or care for the valley dwellers, killing anyone who disagreed with him. But for whatever reason her father worshipped him. She would always loathe him, he was the reason they were stuck here on this island and never able to leave. All transportation off the island ran during the day, so unless she was willing to risk her life and stow away in a shipping container, she could never leave. A risk she had considered on more than one occasion. Witches occasionally aided the transport of vampires to the island but leaving required permission from Zagan, and he only allowed vampires to leave the island to bring trade or more vampires back.

If the sun didn't restrict her to the east side of the island all day she might enjoy the island life a bit more, but between the old-style witches, who were as ugly on the inside as the dark magic they possessed, and the pompous vampires, she didn't have very many options on the friend front. Forced to live her immortal life as a slave to the sun on an island that gave her nothing. She stared at the dark clouds covering the valley as she descended the side of the volcano into the bellows of the sunless valley.

Eternally stuck.

Staring at her jewelry box, Dori picked up different necklaces and looked in the mirror, overthinking her outfit and her plans for the night. It had been a while since Dori had been out to a place like the Dragon Lounge. She normally spent her nights studying, sewing or hanging in Zalor with fairies. Any fairy would caution her from leaving the realm at night. But something a little rebellious could do her some good.

Dori slid one hanger after the other to the left as she looked through her closet to try and figure out something to wear. Being indecisive was not helping her at this moment; she turned back and glanced at her sewing machine and the case full of fabric stored below the tiny corner desk it sat on. She wished she put more time into making some of the clothes she had already designed, but she did all she could to escape this house. Dori rarely spent any time here, especially if her little brother wasn't here. She had sports, clubs, plenty of friends, and a boyfriend; she had plenty of reasons to be anywhere other than here.

And yet, she longed for this room to feel like a safe space. Her room was small, like any other space in the house, nestled in the corner of the second floor right next to her brothers' room, and across from her parents room. Downstairs was more spacious, with a large, cozy living room next to a little dining area and a tiny kitchen that Dori's mother had been wanting to renovate for years.

The house was on the south of the island, atop a hill above the Water fairy village. Dori had long admired that village, where all fairy homes were inside large shells and coral arranging the small neighborhood leading to the Azure beach with it's magnificent blue sand. Dori wished she lived there and often found herself there when she ran away from the chaos at home. The little hill with only a few homes seemed normal compared to the magnificence of living in seashells.

The Teresi's house was nestled inside a large blue blossom tree, and nearly blended in with it. Still, it had features similar to a human home; wood paneling, small patio, white shutters, and large window leading into the family room. She longed for a home, a place she truly felt she could come back to and feel secure. But she was about to start senior year at Zalor High. After that she could leave. Be free. She wasn't quite sure where she was going yet, but all that mattered is she wasn't staying here.

She turned back around to focus on her getting out tonight. She kept flipping through the clothes and came to her shiny royal purple top.

"Perfect," she said in triumph, "This and my black skirt, with my little black boots... Winner!" She exclaimed. Her joy was brief though as she removed the purple top from its hanger and the next thing in her closet was the orange top she was just thinking about earlier today. She tried to fight it but this house held too much power over her, and the memory clouded her mind.

Dori walked down the stairs and saw her younger brother crying in the corner. As she approached the base of the stairs she saw her older brother had backed her mother against the wall and was screaming at her. Before Dori could fully grasp the scene and determine her next steps, Jareth raised his hand and brought it down swiftly across their mother's face.

Dori gasped. "HEY!" She yelled involuntarily, not having any plan of what she would do next.

Jareth turned and faced her. "What do you want?" he yelled in response. "This has nothing to do with you!" he screamed.

Dori was terrified but refused to let anything more happen to her mother, and who knew what had already happened to her little brother. "Blythe, go upstairs to my room please." She said without taking her eyes off Jareth.

Blythe raised his head from his knees. Dori briefly looked at her younger brother and nodded, quickly turning her attention back to Jareth. Blythe got up off the floor and walked quickly behind his sister and scurried up the stairs.

"Why do you always stick your nose where it doesn't belong?" Jareth asked as he approached her.

Dori wanted to back up and keep the distance between them but wouldn't grant him the satisfaction of her appearing afraid. She was used to standing up to him but this was the first time she stood in the way of his physical aggression, usually their dad was around when he got physical. "Whatever is going on, we can handle it in a better way."

"What does it matter to you? You weren't here so you have no business getting involved now."

"I'm not going to stand aside while you assault my mother," Dori asserted. Adelyn stood paralyzed still holding her reddened cheek.

"*Our* mother." Jareth corrected.

"She deserves respect; if you can't even show her a speck of decency then you don't deserve to call her *mom.*"

"Why do you think you're so much better than me! You are a worthless little brat!" Jareth kept yelling calling Dori all kinds of names, as his hands began to glow orange with the fire of the anger he had towards her.

"Jareth, please." Adelyn whimpered.

"Stay out of this," Jareth barked at his mother. As he faced Dori again his eyes were glowing shades of red and orange.

"Jareth, try and take a deep breath." Dori said calmly. She had seen him this angry but he never displayed his power in this way, she feared he would completely lose control.

But of course, Dori's directions pushed him to do exactly that.

Fire poured out of each of Jareth's hands as he screamed uncontrollably. He kept yelling profanity at Dori and their mother igniting the living room in flames. Dori ran to her mother and the two Meta fairies were able to channel enough power to create a dimensional barrier to try and contain the flames. Together they were able to create a globe surrounding Jareth, the flames created a vicious vortex within. It was a thin force field, a strong feat for just two Meta fairies, so they could feel the intense heat coming from within it. The orange and red consumed the entire globe blocking their view of Jareth in the middle.

The overuse of his magic overloaded Jareth quickly, and the barrier his sister and mother created pushed him too far. The flames went out as Jareth lost consciousness and fell to the floor. Dori nearly fell over herself as she too was drained after using so much power. She keeled over resting her hands on her knees and took a few deep breaths.

Adelyn ran to her son and made sure he was okay. He was burned but breathing well. She turned to her daughter, "Come over here and heal his burns."

Dori still catching her breath looked up at her mother, "He will be fine."

"He will be better if he wakes up not in pain from all these burns."

"You have the same powers that I do, you can heal him and I will go check on Blythe," Dori stood up protesting and began to walk toward the stairs.

Adelyn stopped her. "You sent him over the edge, you should heal him."

Dori stood frozen, her thoughts burning as hot as the living room was a few minutes ago. There was no use having the same argument she'd had plenty of times before. Dori's Meta side was from her mom; Adelyn was a strong fairy who worked along side the council as one of the realm's healers. She had a passion for helping other people, and was really good at it, but that passion often came at a price. Adelyn seemed to take care of everyone except herself, and she struggled deeply. Dori and her mom's relationship had been strained many years earlier when she fell ill and Dori was forced to help take care of things around the house in her absence. She felt like an adult in the house because she had had to act like one for so long. She did all she could to help her mother stay together, which was why she always stepped in the way when Jareth got out of hand. Jareth despised her, so she fueled his rage. And keeping the peace in her house meant taking the brunt of that rage and then taking the blame for it. She exhaled and walked toward her unconscious brother lying on the floor, he was definitely more tolerable in this state.

CHAPTER 3

Touching the velvety orange blouse between her fingers Dori hoped maybe one day she would be able to wear it again. But every time she looked at it she still saw that orange and red globe and relived the first time he set the house ablaze.

She took a step back from her closet and closed the protection charm around it. Ever since that day she figured out a way to protect parts of her room, she wish she could just put a charm around her entire room, but it needed to remain a secret. Having a dimensional charm in her room would not go over well, with her strict father or her nosy brother. Only she and Blythe knew. Sometimes he would use her closet to hide in, the spacial charm created a barrier where even if someone was looking there was no way to find him without knowing the key to the charm.

Dori put on a purple top and black skirt; grabbed some jewelry to add some flare, a few sparkling beaded bracelets and a dainty necklace with shimmering rhinestones spaced out on the thin chain. She looked at herself in the mirror with approval before she grabbed a sweatshirt and tossed it over her outfit before heading downstairs. She tossed her hair up in a bun while walking down the stairs to really sell it. Her parents were relaxing on the couch in the living room.

"I'm headed out to hang with some friends." Dori said to her parents.

"Okay," her dad said. "Don't be out too late, and stay in the city. No need going out of the realm at night," he added.

"Bye, sweetie." Her mom said.

She gave their bronze dog a quick pet on the head and kissed her squished-in nose as she moved swiftly down to the foyer and out the door before Jareth could crawl out of his cave. And as soon as she stepped out the door she breathed in the cool night air.

Now she just had to make it to the portal without anyone seeing her leave the realm.

Dori had arrived to the Dragon Lounge before Mae, which made her feel a little more awkward being out in the beach town after dusk. She looked in the window as she approached the club; there was a band on the stage and people dancing the night away. With only a couple weeks left in the summer season there were plenty of tourists around the island still. In a month the beach towns would appear abandoned. It was actually nice; most of the locals knew about the supernatural so there wasn't as much sneaking around. Plus the off season with all the festivals and holidays were loads of fun and more like living in a small town, which was a wonderful change of pace from living in the biggest city in the fae realm.

Mae seemed to magically appear right behind Dori. "Hey," she said, tapping her on the shoulder.

Dori turned around a little startled, "Oh, hey!" She looked at the other girl, wearing loose ripped jeans and a black top. She felt a little overdressed and was a little jealous of how good she looked in such a simple outfit.

They smiled at each other. "Cute outfit! You've been here before right?" Mae asked.

The compliment reassured her of the clothing choice. "Not during the summer, and only for a special event," Dori answered, shrugging a bit.

"Oh! Well the bands are always amazing here and the food is fantastic!"

"Dude, I'm always up for food!" Dori smiled.

"Sweet. Let's go!"

They walked in the door and were greeted with some intense electric guitar and heavy drums, the singer on the stage grabbed the mic and wailed into it. Dori had only ever been in Dragon Lounge during the day where the decorative dragons on every wall and surface were delicate pastel colors, but now they glowed in neon colors enhanced by the black-lights that circled the room.

Dori looked at Mae, mouth gaping open. "Already loving this."

Mae smiled, "Wait 'til you try their food!"

Mae ordered her food quickly, telling Dori how she always got the same thing. Dori sat there a bit embarrassed by her indecisiveness and just ordered the same as Mae. Dori suggested honey lavender limeade, a fairy favorite. Mae declined and stuck with water, leaving Dori uncomfortable as she sipped on her purple drink with frilly flower garnish. They sat their awkwardly, mostly in silence until the food arrived.

Dori attempted to pick up her burger and it slid right out of the buns and made an aggressive plop noise on her plate. Her cheeks turned bright red, but the two laughed and it finally broke the tension. They sat there talking about their favorite bands and foods. Once they cleared their plates Mae dragged Dori to the dance floor. Dori loved dancing but her dance moves were chaotic, so she only moved when her eyes were shut and she embraced the music. She felt free and, with eyes still shut, kept moving to the music trying her best not to think about the weird looks she was probably getting.

Mae pushed her way to the front of the crowd when one of her favorite songs came on, dragging Dori along behind her. Mae sang out the words at the base of the stage as the band sang it back to them. Dori sang the words she knew while Mae belted it out word for word. The band loved Mae's energy and pulled her up on stage. Mae spent the next song hyping up the crowd to dance along with them. Meanwhile, Dori stared from amidst the crowd, trying not to get lost in the bustle of people fawning over Mae. Mae was totally in her element and Dori began to feel more like background noise, but kept a smile and occasionally continued dancing to any of the songs she knew.

Mae seemed to be really well known here. Dori thought more about what that could mean about the identity of her new friend. She was either an extremely brave fairy who spent many nights outside of the realm, or she wasn't a fairy at all. She anxiously chewed on her lip again wondering if she were a lost fae, she knew she sensed light about her but her aura gave off so many mixed signals.

As the band finished up, Dori needed to get some air and Mae followed; she wasn't going to let her go out and face any number of vampires skulking around outside. They walked down to the beach. Dori stood there amazed at the view of the stars. There wasn't much light pollution coming from the island, so the night sky was illuminated with sparkles. Closing her eyes, she inhaled the cool breeze of the ocean air closing her eyes, allowing serenity to flow through her, then exhaled smiling.

Mae smirked watching her new friend. Then it hit her, if she was indeed a fairy, she probably never got to see the island at night. Of course she hadn't really been to the Dragon Lounge, vampires flooded the towns at night, especially during the tourist season, and a pretty young fairy wouldn't last two minutes on her own. Mae felt a little bad for her friend, then felt kind of impressed that she agreed to meet her tonight in the first place.

The duo walked down to the water. They both let the waves come crashing on their now bare feet. Dori was soaking in every second of the night, and Mae looked at her in wonder.

"Why did you decide to come tonight?" Mae asked.

Dori looked up at her a little surprised. "Well, we had a nice time talking this morning. And it's kind of refreshing to spend time with someone who doesn't expect anything from you," Dori said honestly, looking back toward the ocean.

"What do you mean?"

"Everyone that knows me expects me to be one thing or another, and I just want space to breathe lately."

Mae nodded. "Yeah, I totally get what you mean. Feeling trapped in everyone else's view of you."

"Exactly. You seemed to be really well known at the lounge too," Dori said.

Mae smirked looking down at the waves hitting her toes. "Yeah, but again, everyone expects me to be this particular person, and I just want to let loose," she looked up at her new friend, "and honestly you let me do that."

"I did?"

Mae chuckled. "Definitely! You're so free on the dance floor and I didn't feel like I needed to look a specific way or anything. It was a nice break from my group of *friends*."

Dori smiled. "Yeah when it comes to dancing I really just don't care. And again, no one knew me there so it really didn't matter."

"I'm glad you wanted to meet up again," Mae added.

"I'm not usually good at making new friends, so I was scared to ask," Dori said honestly.

"Well I'm really glad you did," Mae said smiling, "What does your week look like? Maybe we can get together again?"

"Yeah, absolutely! Maybe in a quiet setting so we talk more? Get to know each other?"

Mae nodded, "Sounds nice." She thought for a minute, "There's this coffee shop on the North side of the island called Bitter Brew Box," she stuttered over the alliteration. Few vampires, and even fewer people knew about the tempered glass that was on the windows of the coffee shop, and with a back entrance available through some covered passageways Mae was able to get there and back without hitting sun rays, if she timed it right.

Dori laughed and attempted to say it herself. They both repeated the name and laughed as they pronounced the words carefully to say it properly. "Okay, I will meet you there tomorrow morning," Dori said as she pulled her phone out of her pocket to check the time. "It is getting late, so I should get back home. But I will see you maybe around 9?" She asked.

Mae nodded. "Here let me see your phone," she reached out her hand, grabbing her friend's phone. She added her number in the contacts; then she turned and took a selfie with Dori with the ocean in the back glistening in the moonlight and set it as her contact photo. "Text me when you get home okay."

Dori took her phone back and smiled, admiring the photo. "And you do the same."

Mae smiled and they went their separate ways, or so she made Dori believe. She would've liked to walk her home, but her home was probably in the other realm, so that wasn't even possible. Passing from shadow to shadow, Mae trailed her friend, ever watchful against the fangs of the night. She wasn't sure why she felt so protective over this girl she just met, but there was something about their connection that made her feel so alive again.

Following her new friend through the shimmering pink trees of Dragonwood, along the moonlight dappled paths, Mae watched Dori approach the small waterfall at the edge of the forest. Mae waited, observing with wonder as her friend placed a hand on the side of the mountain next to the rushing water and vanished into the rocks, disappearing into the fae realm.

"So that's how that works," she whispered to herself.

She would have to be up pretty early to get to passageways in the north before the sun rose, so she headed back to the Cano Valley to get some sleep.

CHAPTER 4

D ori got out of bed and packed her bag for the day. Swim suit, in case she decided to hit the beach, a book, and some snacks. Abigor was off doing trainings with new recruits and Blythe was hanging with some friends so she had the day to herself. Since she was meeting Mae at the North part of the island she decided she would make a day of it. If Mae was free she would spend it with her, if not then she would explore and enjoy the beach since she only had so much longer to do so.

It was her dad's day off, so he was sitting at the table drinking his cappuccino when she reached the bottom of the stairs.

"Good morning," Cyrus said to his daughter, calmly as he took a sip from his mug.

"Morning, Dad," Dori said giving him a smile.

"Where were you last night?" Cyrus asked. Dori held her breath a moment before he continued. "I don't set many rules with you, Endora, but I was pretty clear when I asked you not to stay out too late."

"I'm sorry. I lost track of time," she apologized hoping he wouldn't pry too much. She never snuck out so she didn't know how to do this whole thing, she never had to lie to her dad and felt uneasy about being deceitful.

"You're lucky your mother went to sleep early and didn't notice, you know how worried she gets when you kids are out late."

"I know. I don't mean to worry her," she said genuinely. Her mother may be a worrywart but Dori hated increasing any of her negative thoughts, she had enough as it is. Dori looked at her father, searching for how upset he actually was with her.

Dori inherited her father's fiery spirit, while Blythe was like a carbon copy of their father with less fire, and more hair; then there was Jareth, who looked just like their mother but augmented the fiery spirit and turned it to pure rage. Cyrus had a temper and Dori feared it at times, but they had a true friendship and bonded over things like singing and sports, and every now and then she received that daddy's-little-girl treatment. Of her parents, Dori's father definitely understood her more, even if she mostly took after her mother. But in the past few years she felt the increasing pressure to meet his "golden child" expectations of her. With Jareth failing out of school the year before, Dori's school and future had taken center stage and she hated the extra pressure that brought. Dori's passion for creating clothes was admired and encouraged by her father, but never seen as a potential career choice, and that hurt her deeply. Cyrus felt Dori needed to pursue a career with more stability. While it came from a good place and he wanted his daughter to be well cared for but all Dori wanted was a good support system so she could pursue the things she loved.

"I know you want to enjoy the last days of summer, but you cannot forget your responsibilities. Your senior year starts in just over a week and you've got a lot of work to do," her father said.

"I know, Dad. I already have most of my electives picked out and my schedule nailed down. I am going to submit the paperwork tomorrow. I really do have to go though," she said as she kissed her father on the cheek and began to walk away.

"Oh, I already finished that up for you," her father replied.

Dori stopped abruptly, her thoughts holding in a frustrated scream as she turned back to him. "What do you mean you finished it? I hadn't filled out my entire schedule yet."

"I know. I took care of that, and you had selected some odd classes too. 'The Intricacies of Water', why would you want to take that?" He asked with genuine confusion at what possible purpose the class could have for her.

"I love the ocean and the way water feels——wait, what do you mean you took care of it? What did you submit?" She questioned a little heatedly.

"If you are going to intern at the tower next summer before studying under the council you will need a much better course layout than 'Celebrations of Harvest' and 'Creativity in Magic'," Cyrus added.

"You removed those from my schedule? Without asking me? I don't even know if I want to intern at the tower. I might not even declare my faction at graduation."

Dori began to freak out internally, her heart racing and her brain stuttered over her frustrations.

Cyrus looked at her unbelieving. "Of course you will be interning! Your Sun magic is by far superior to *anyone* in your class. Plus, you have proved yourself one of the strongest Meta fairies Zalor has seen in ages. Why would you defer entering your faction?"

"The other magics interest me," she said, shrugging as if the fact should already be known. Not that either of her parents ever listened to her when it came to doing anything other than what they had planned.

The faction system was put in place nearly two millennia ago. The realm was divided into one faction for each type of magic: Dryad, Tempes, Night, Sun, Water, Fauna, and Meta. Each fairy must choose a singular faction, only practicing one magic for their life; though they were permitted to have a secondary magic to help aid their primary magic. Since the worlds were divided and fairies were directed to fade into myth, interaction with humans became increasingly limited, and the 7 factions were divided into two categories, Gregarious and Solidarity. Meta and Fauna fairies are more likely to interact with humans than any other kind of fairy, as some of their empowerment comes through emotions, auras, and life-force. Water was the only other Gregarious. The other 4 factions were Solidarity and mainly stayed within the fae realm unless preforming specific duties, like Tempes initiating the season changes, or Dryads nurturing the planet.

Whether Gregarious or Solidarity, all fairies are directed to stay hidden from humankind and keep up the ruse that they are fictional creatures. Any interaction with humans was to be in human appearance, which any fairy is able to transform into. The diminutive sprite form gave all fairies the ability to fly, however any fairies could shift from sprite to human scale keeping their natural form; human form allowed them to blend into the world and appear relatively ordinary.

Dori took a breath to calm herself before continuing. "I think I want to go to school and try my hand at each of them. If I am meant to be a Meta fairy—or Sun," she added in hopes of not agitating him more. "Then I will be. But, I don't even know what my secondary magic will be. Plus I still think the faction system is so—confining." As the words left her mouth Dori knew she had said too much.

The only one in her family she could talk to about exploring other magics was Blythe, who shared her thoughts on being confined to one magic for your entire life. Cyrus didn't mind much that Dori pursued her talents in Meta, but he thought she would have more success pursuing Sun. Meta fairies were scarce nowadays, and the jobs and roles they played in their society were nowhere near as well regarded as those filled by the Sun faction. Her dad made this opinion known, and often, as he was convinced it was the most practical way to ensure her future was concrete and stable. She understood, she did - but it still grated on her, it still hurt. There was no room to be a magic nomad.

"Confining? Endora, the faction system has kept our people safe for centuries. The fae live longer, prosper, and stay safe in the sanctity of this realm *because* of this system!" Her father began to raise his voice, his face and head turning a shade of red.

She needed to back track even if she wanted to fight her way out of this one. "That's not what I meant. I just feel like I'm not ready," Dori said, hoping that would do.

"Well, you have a year. Then you will be ready. Your people need you."

Dori nodded, biting the inside of her cheek to prevent her voice from raging out of her throat like the voice inside her head was eager to do. "Do you have a copy of my schedule?"

Cyrus walked to the other side of the room and grabbed a piece of paper and handed it to his daughter. "I took these classes too, they will be a great help to you, I promise. You'll find your way this year, and you will be great at it."

"Thanks, dad. I'll be out for the day, beach and library, the usual," Dori took the paper and walked toward the door.

But before she was able to reach for the knob, Jareth came out of his room. "Hey, what's going on out here?"

"Nothing, Jareth."

"Did I hear you mention the beach? I have been wanting to go and would love to tag along," Jareth said. He always loved to invite himself to places, as if they were friends and he wasn't always telling her how she was a useless waste of space.

"I'm meeting a friend, not sure what our plan is," Dori remarked, trying to hide her contempt.

"Wait, you have friends?" Jareth scoffed. "Let's get Blythe and we can all go. Your friend wouldn't mind your brothers tagging along, right?" Jareth said mockingly.

"She might, actually, girl time and all," Dori said, a sure-fire way to escape a conversation with Jareth. "Next time though!" Dori said with a smile as she walked out the door. Her smile fell as soon as she hit the front yard. She hated when he invited himself everywhere, maybe if he was the nice brother he claimed to be, she would take him places. She was always bringing Blythe along on her adventures, but they were best friends, and she would do anything to escape time with Jareth.

Letting out a deep exhale, Dori flitted into sprite form. Gliding towards the north of the city, she glared at the tower as she flew passed, she felt as if it was glaring back at her, a reminder of the life she was being forced into. Flying straight through the waterfalls behind the tower she came out in her human form on the other side. Always best to travel through the portals in human form so no one spotted a little winged thing in the forest.

She turned around and admired the waterfall from this side. It was so small compared to the towering one on the other side. But the water glittered with all the magic held behind it. Dori rarely traveled through this portal, not for any particular reason, she just didn't travel to North Beach much.

Mae was already in the café when Dori walked in. Dori looked to the left at the wide array of beverage options written on black boards hanging on the glittering black brick wall. She looked around at the coffee shop, there were antique tables and chairs, a bar with red velvet barstools. Towards the back there was a loft with a black tree trunk staircase and towers of bookshelves lining the back wall. She loved the dark feel of the place, it was obviously one of the supernatural-themed locations on the island, designed with a vampire aesthetic.

Dori thought for a moment about her friend suggesting this location, but there was no way she could be a vampire. They were meeting here during the day, after all, so Dori dismissed the thought.

Maybe she is supernatural, but like a witch or a banshee. Dori said to herself, hoping she was a witch. Dori thought the Seraphina got a bad rap. Just because their ancestors were a power hungry coven doesn't mean the witches on the island today were all bad. She had talked to a handful in town before and they were really nice; the woman who owned the shop by Siren's cove really knew her stuff. It wasn't always a bad thing to associate with them, but affiliations with lost fae was customarily frowned upon. Plus, depending on what type of lost fae she was she could be a real danger. Dori shook the thought from her head, remembering the light Mae's energy gives off. *No way she could be that dark*, she thought.

Dori and Mae met at the counter giving each other a simple 'Hello' and 'Good Morning'.

"I might need a minute to decide," Dori said looking back up at the menu boards. "There are so many options."

Mae smiled. "Try to keep it simple for Conrad though, he's not so great at the complex stuff," Mae said, mocking at the barista behind the counter.

"How would you know, you always order the same simple thing. Iced Mocha Mint in the summer and hot cocoa when it's colder." Conrad smiled sharply at Mae before turning toward Dori, his entire demeanor shifting. "Hi,

I'm Conrad," he said, flashing his pearly white smile in a half grin.

"Dori," she said smiling. "Well, I'm always up for new things! But I like my coffee extra sweet, so whatever you recommend," Dori said.

"Alright, I got you. Anything for breakfast?"

"A red velvet muffin sounds good."

"You got it, gorgeous," Conrad said, playfully.

Dori couldn't help but blush at the handsome blonde complimenting her. She couldn't ignore his charming smile and sparkling green eyes. He had been nicer to her in the two minutes since she stepped in this café than Abigor had in months. She pushed that thought back and paid for her order.

"I'll take a bagel with butter and my iced mocha," Mae cut in with a saucy attitude.

"Of course you will," Conrad returned the sass. "They will be right up," he said to them both.

Mae walked toward the back of the café and Dori followed. She sat at a table next to the tall window with the staircase to the loft a few feet away on the other side. Mae loved coming here because it was the only place she could see the day pass by. She was almost losing herself in the view before she remembered she had company today and Dori sat across from her.

"So you come here often, huh?" Dori asked.

Mae chuckled a bit. "Yeah it's my regular place. I come here a couple times a week."

"I have a place like that too," Dori said. "But it's nothing like this place! I love the theme. And the tower of books and the loft is so cool! Plus my regular coffee shop is always so packed," she said with a deep sigh. "You can't really talk with anyone without everyone around eavesdropping."

Mae sat back in her chair and kicked her feet up on the chair next to her. "Yeah, it's nice and quiet here. Not a lot of people know about it, but that's not such a bad thing." Mae smiled

"Order up!" Conrad shouted from behind the bar.

Mae began to take her feet off the chair next to her but Dori jumped up and gave her a quick "I got it," and Mae put her feet back in surprise. She thanked Dori as she returned with the tray.

Mae took a sip of her mocha and looked at Dori. "Alright, friend—" she said, drawing out the word, "what's your story?"

Dori was sipping her mug of whatever Conrad made her. It had notes of hazelnut and nutmeg, a hint of honey, and was topped with frothy milk with an espresso sprinkling in the shape of a moon and star. She set down the mug after admiring the taste of her beverage and looked at Mae, thinking a moment.

"I don't really know how to answer that," Dori chuckled as she pulled off a piece of her muffin and ate it. "Well, I start my senior year of high school this year," but as she said that she remembered her conversation with her dad and paused a little too long.

"Well that's a start I guess," Mae looked at her quizzically.

"Sorry, I was just remembering something about my schedule for the semester." Mae looked at her as if offering the floor. Dori exhaled and continued. "I had some really fun classes picked out and was excited about this year, but I just found out this morning that my dad changed my classes. I haven't even had a chance to look at what classes he picked for me," Dori said. She slid her schedule out of her bag sitting on the table between them, but the first class, Sun Fairies IV Honors, quickly caught her eye. Dori reached back into her bag pretending to be looking for something and grabbed the first thing to cover up the papers. She awkwardly smiled holding up her chapstick as her swim coverup sat overtop of her schedule. Applying her chapstick, she shoved everything back in her bag, then placed it on the floor to avoid any more close calls. Dori lifted her mug to her face trying to hide her anxiety, the warm beverage helped soothe her.

Mae jumped in, "Sounds a bit controlling, like my dad."

"It's like he is and isn't. He has these great dreams for my life but he wants me to go down this path I'm not sure I want to."

"Like what?" Mae asked.

Dori thought about how she could explain it in a vague enough way to not talk about the fae council. "He always says he wants the best for me, but his best is following in his footsteps and wanting me to pursue some career with a concrete holding. Yah know? Like if you go into medicine or business then you're always bound to have a safety net. But I like art and creating and still want to figure out what I want to do, but being an artist of any kind is risky."

"So you don't get to follow your own dreams?"

"No, not really," Dori said somberly as she sipped her coffee again. "This is really good."

Mae smiled, "Good." Mae paused a moment. "So what about your mom? Does she encourage your dreams?"

"It's really weird. Like she loves the stuff I make and always tells me how skilled I am and wants me to be happy but then just follows whatever my dad says."

"Dude, my mom is the same way!" Mae exclaimed sitting up.

"It sucks! And my brothers don't get the same thing because I am the one with the straight A's and work ethic. So they are encouraged to do their best but my best needs to be better."

"Right, like it's never enough for them. Wait, so you have brothers too?" Mae asked.

"Yeah two, one older, one younger," Dori replied.

"Stop, so do I!" Mae blurted.

They both looked at each other, jaws dropping for a moment before laughing and going back to their breakfast.

"Do you get along with your brothers?" Dori asked.

"For the most part," Mae said before biting into the last of her bagel. "We have our ups and downs but we aren't super close anymore. Kinda like how your dad wants you to follow in his footsteps, my brothers kinda followed my dad's and I just don't want to." Mae looked down.

Dori grabbed another sip of her coffee, then looked at the comfy chairs and couches toward the back of the café. Her eyes went upward toward the gorgeous black bookcases in the cozy loft. "Hey, do you wanna continue this in the comfy chairs in the loft?"

Mae smirked. "Sure! I'll bring up the dishes and meet you up there."

Dori walked up the swirling staircase and felt a distant spark of the magic the tree once possessed. She felt a surge of energy as she felt the intricate details of the wood beneath her hand. Then all she felt was glee as she took another sip of her coffee and looked at the wide array of books surrounding the loft. She ran her fingers across the covers, briefly examining the context. Dori had a hard time reading, she loved losing herself in a book but her struggle getting through text was always an excuse not to read often. Her thoughts trailed off thinking about the swimming letters on a page, and was determined to work on reading more.

She was still perusing the books when Mae came up the stairs. Mae smiled as she brought her straw to her lips and plopped on a black arm chair, kicking her feet up on the merlot colored ottoman in front of her. She watched her friend a moment and then continued their previous conversation.

"So do you and your brothers not get along?" Mae questioned.

Dori turned from the stack of books toward her friend and sat in a bowl chair that hung from the ceiling. "My little brother is my best friend; we look out for each other. But my older brother..." She took a long pause and Mae looked at her, concerned. "Well, let's just say he's a bad person."

"I don't have anywhere to go today. Feel free to say more," Mae said as she slouched back in her chair a bit more, taking another swig of her drink.

Dori's eyes glossed over a bit. "He has anger issues," she said simply. "Like I don't get it! He just freaks out sometimes over the smallest things," Dori continued, becoming frustrated. "He will be fine and pretend to be the friendly older brother but then be screaming in your face hours later. He has absolutely no remorse for what he does, like he doesn't even remember how awful he is," Dori let out a big sigh, closing her eyes, breathing in slow, trying to calm herself again to keep her memories at bay.

Mae sat up a bit, feeling the seriousness of the conversation. "I'm sorry. I might know a bit of what you mean. My dad sounds like the same kind of person."

Dori looked up at her friend. "It's hard. And I've kinda become the peacekeeper in the house, yah know? Protecting my little brother and mom, deflecting his anger and trying to keep things calm." Dori shook her head. "But I feel like if I express myself at all it's an offense, and anything I do aggravates him because I am always standing up to him. Do you know what I mean?" She looked at Mae with sorrow deep in her eyes.

"Absolutely," Mae said reaching out toward her friend. "Pretty much exactly how you feel." Mae knew they could keep talking but hated seeing that sorrow fill her friend's eyes. "I think it was fate you were in my spot yesterday."

Dori gave a small laugh and joy returned to her eyes, joining the sorrow still staining them. "Yeah, I think so too."

CHAPTER 5

D ori stood against a wall eyes tightly shut.

"You are worthless!" Jareth yelled, almost spitting in her face. "All you do is cause chaos. You will never amount to anything! You are stupid and WEAK," he screamed.

Dori opened her eyes and stared at Jareth, whose face was mere inches from hers. Her heart screamed back *'No'* and *'Shut up'* but when she opened her mouth she had no voice.

Jareth's mouth contorted into a creep's smile "What, little sister? You think you can fight me?" He sneered as he pinned her to the wall, his forearm crushing her neck against the wall.

She fought for air, she tried to push him away but it was as if every muscle in her body was weakened. Dori used all her might but could not get her brother off of her. There was no one around to help her. She felt faint as her chest ached from her breathless lungs. Everything turned black.

Gasping for air, Dori shot up from under her covers, as she awoke from her nightmare. She took a moment looking around her room taking deep breaths. Clutching her chest she tried to focus on the air in her lungs, even if it felt like it was being sucked out. She began to calm herself as the nightmare hung over her.

"What a grand way to start the first day of senior year," she said to herself. She walked to her bathroom and began to get ready. She recalled the last nightmare she had as she angrily brushed her teeth. They were getting more frequent now, and more fictitious. She knew she could easily over power her brother, magic or not. She was stronger. He *was* the spineless little coward but for whatever reason these trauma dreams were twisting everything around. It's like they were telling her she would never escape him. She froze at the thought of it.

Dori looked at herself in the mirror, staring blankly into the hazel eyes staring back at her. But as tears started to well in her eyes she pushed everything back, as usual. Of course this only made her physical pain worse. She lifted her shirt and noticed the blueish patch on her right rib getting larger. It started about the size of dime, though the pain behind it covered a much larger area, and now was as large as a peach.

When it had first appeared she thought it was a bruise. Which concerned her at the time because of all the pain she had been having in her abdomen. The last year she had spent a lot of time with the healer fairies and human physicians, but nothing was actually wrong with her. Nothing but the fact she was in excruciating pain on a regular basis. It didn't make sense for a fairy to have an illness like this, if you could even call it that, all she knew was the pain came on at random times and there was nothing she could do to help it. Even her healing magic could only keep the pain back for so long.

Dori focused her healing magic and placed her hand over the spot. Her fingers sparkled with yellow wisps. Closing her eyes, she took a few slow breaths. She removed her hand and opened her eyes again to look at her side. Dori knew it was just superficial aid, like taking a pain killer, but at least for now the pain was at bay and there were no marks.

She did her hair and a bit of makeup. Her usual morning routine was pretty simple. Wearing only bare touches of makeup to match her outfit, and usually leaving her hair to fall in gentle natural waves over her shoulders. Dori loved allowing her natural beauty to shine bright. She tossed on the dark purple shorts and baby blue top she had picked out a week ago. Gathering her backpack and taking one last look in the mirror, she felt confident.

This year was the first year Dori felt she could stand on her own. Abigor had finished the year before last, and Jareth, well, was in last year's class, not that he completed his classes. But she would no longer be Abigor's girlfriend, or Jareth's little sister, flip flopping from being connected to the well-liked and the well-hated. She smiled as Blythe stepped out of the door behind her.

"Ready Doe?" Blythe smiled, calling her by his special nickname. When Jareth was in a chummy mood he would try to adopt the nickname, but Blythe was the only one in the world that Dori allowed to use the endearment.

They transformed and flew across the city together. She was excited to have him in school with her again. Blythe was starting freshman year and wasn't nearly as nervous as she was 3 years ago. He was well-liked in his class and was excited for finally getting to high school.

Dori would turn 18 later this year and her aging would slow. Fairies aged through childhood like humans, but after that it took a fairy 8-10 rotations around the sun to age a year, depending on how powerful the fairy was. Tempes and Dryad fairies were the first ones to discover this ability, since they were the first to focus their magic solely in one type. Blythe would learn more this year about the history that told of King and Queen Amara who were the most powerful fae in each magic, and they were blessed with a child of each. King Kairos directed his children to lead the fae realm as a council of factions instead of royals, to become stronger, have less weaknesses, and be less susceptible to darkness.

Dori still questioned the details of that whole thing. She knew her history well, but she questioned why such a powerful King would want different for his children. King Kairos and Queen Dahlia brought the fae realm into the greatest time in dynasties. Why would they want to limit the powers of their children? They built a strong and powerful kingdom and Dori wondered if they would have handled the divide from the human world differently than the council did, many centuries later.

She and Blythe arrived at Zalor High with a whole fleet of other students. The skies of Zalor looked like it was painted with a glittery rainbow as students from all factions made their way to school. Just past the glistening turquoise waters, Dori's feet landed on the black stone pavement leading to the large arched doors, made from the same blue blossom tree that her house was was tucked in. She turned back, taking in the fresh air before stepping into the halls for her senior year. Dori watched the reflections of dazzling colors glide across the water as her fellow students flooded into the large stone fortress.

As their magic grew, each fairy took on features of their factions. As students with undeclared factions, the young fae of Zalor high took on features of their most powerful magic, with no distinct adaptation features yet. Like Dori's friend, Sage, who came from a long line of Dryads; her hair had begun shifting into a leafy green texture. Although her skin hadn't yet started to take on the appearance of bark like her mother's, some green began to highlight her slender brown face. Tempes fairies often blended in with the weather. One of their sub factions, snow fairies, often had pale blue skin with snowflakes for attire, which is where the name came from. Many Tempes fairies hid amongst the clouds or spent their days sailing along the breeze. Few fairies were caught between two magics, like Dori, and therefore not yet displaying adaptations by senior year of high school; and she had never seen another fairy with purple in their wings.

Dori showed Blythe to the freshman hall where he would have orientation and they would show him around the school. Then she went to her locker. Her friend, Lily, whose locker was right next to hers this year, was already at her locker decorating it with some floral stickers and pastel accessories. There was no question what magic Lily excelled in; her natural bronze hair began to sprout flowers last year, crowning her head in hues of gentle pink, and her hands always had coils of vines around them stemming from up her arms. She lived and breathed Dryad, waiting for the day she could join the sub faction of Flora fairies who handled all the flowering wonders of the world.

"Morning, Lily!" Dori said excitedly.

"Dori! Where have you been?" Lily questioned. "You've been M.I.A. for the past couple weeks," she added.

"I've been visiting North Beach," Dori paused for a moment thinking about her new friend and the coffee shop she wanted to keep a secret. "Just exploring and interacting with tourists before the summer season ends," she gave a wry smile.

"Oh, charging up on Meta power before classes begin?" Lily asked.

Dori thought about how that actually made sense, even if it filled the air with a sense of mockery, and just went with it. "Yup! Gotta be ready for Advanced MetaPhysics," she said, faking a smile as she opened her locker. She had completely forgotten to bring anything for her locker to start the new year. Placing her backpack inside she reached in twisting her fingers and with the flick of her wrist pulled out a little mirror, a couple photos of her with Blythe and friends, and a print out of the handsome blue-eyed vampire from her favorite TV show.

"I'm sure you'll do fine. You're always top of the Meta classes. Keep it up and you'll end up as Meta-valedictorian," Lily joked, knowing her friend had enough on her plate without having to lead the Meta class in graduation and write some dumb speech. Zalor high really pushed the divide of the factions by having one valedictorian per faction, and Dori wanted no part of that. She tried to stay in the background at school, and no matter how good her grades were or how powerful she became in her Meta magic, she really didn't want to be valedictorian and have to get up on stage in front of the entire city. Graduation from Zalor high was a big deal in the city; there was an entire month of festivities surrounding it— parades, parties, magic demonstrations—the works. The entire city gathered to honor the next generation of fairies moving up in the realm. Some fairies would even travel from different parts of the world to see the rising stars of the fae world. Some students getting recruited for positions all over the globe.

"Oh, yay me," Dori said sarcastically. Lily gave her a little pat on the shoulder before flitting off to class. If Dori was Meta-valedictorian then she would have to declare her faction at graduation, and it would be 'disrespectful' to her teachers, the system, and her family if she refused the honor of the highest ranking in her class. Not to mention her dad probably wouldn't let her pass that up since it would guarantee her a slot in the internship in the tower this summer.

She let out a stressful sigh as she opened her locker. Too much to think about on the first day, and she didn't have to worry about Advanced Metaphysics until tomorrow. She was only able to get back into one elective her father switched her out of but she was stuck in classes like 'Council History', and 'Factions and Sub-sects'. For now she grabbed her notebooks and got ready for her first class, 'Sun Fairies IV Honors', another one she was dreading. She was hoping to be done with Sun fairy classes. She knew all she wanted to and this class was to prepare fairies for joining the Sun faction; the last thing she wanted. But of course it was what her father wanted so it was probably the very first class he selected when changing her schedule. Her locker was barely shut when someone bumped into her knocking her books to the floor.

"Oooops," said a tall dark girl with fiery orange hair, turning back to watch Dori pick her books up off the ground.

Kenina.

Dori eyed her school nemesis who had made it her life's work to torment Dori any chance she got. Kenina took every chance she could to belittle Dori, ever since Dori won an award in fae scouts when they were little.

"Good to see you, Dori." Kenina taunted, "Where's your brother? He didn't feel like giving senior year another go?"

Dori kept her head down, grabbing her books.

"Probably for the best. We don't need another year of Fire-face Teresi," scoffed the ditzy girl next to her, that Kenina toted around like a purse.

"Yeah we don't need another cafeteria rebuild," Kenina laughed.

Last year, when Jareth lost his cool on a couple guys at lunch, they had to close off a third of the cafeteria to repair the burnt floors and replace the torched tables. Dori stood just staring at the wicked girl before her.

Kenina beamed with pride at Dori's lack of response. "Well, enjoy your spirit classes, or whatever it is you Meta fairies study," she sneered as both girls flipped their hair and turned to walk away. They continued talking about Jareth as they sauntered off, about a time he called the one girl fat then asked her out two days later. Dori stood silent, cloaked in her embarrassment.

Sage emerged from a vine in the open archway across from Dori's locker, transforming from a small figure that blended with the foliage, to a short elegant beauty with long dark curls.

"She really needs to get over the fae scouts thing," Sage said with a smile.

Dori gave a chuckle, "Yeah maybe in a hundred years or so."

"Let me see your schedule," Sage asked, holding a hand out.

Dori sighed and slipped a paper out of her notebook.

"Ooh, your dad really did a number on your electives. But hey we have flying together!"

Dori took her schedule back, giving a small smile. "Good, I'll need someone on my team to beat the jocks in janberry ball," she said, ignoring the pit in her stomach about the stressful class list.

"Looking forward to it," Sage said, locking arms with Dori as they began to walk down the hall.

The sweet moment was soiled with the sight of her nemesis again as she walked into Sun Fairy Honors.

"Sweet fragile Endora, I thought you were done with fire classes?" Kenina scoffed.

"Then who would you cheat off of for exams, Kenina?" Dori responded with equal disdain, she was feeling a little sassy and decided to roll with it.

"For the last time, it's Nina now. And I would only cheat off you if I wanted to fail," she retorted and turned to the friends surrounding her to laugh with her.

"Right," Dori said, rolling her eyes as she walked past the girl and sat toward the back of the classroom.

"Hello class," Professor Branton said as he walked into the classroom, the smell of sulfur following him. There was no question Branton was a Sun fairy, being hundreds of years old many of his features showed his faction well. Pointed ears and blazing orange eyes, but the most obvious features being his lengthy orange beard and hair, wisping like flickering flames.

Even sitting in the back of the classroom Dori couldn't help but let out a slight cough. Most Sun fairies could embrace all that came with the fiery nature, but Dori dealt with it enough at home and could never stand the smell of smoke. It reminded her too much of the remains of her home after one of Jareth's fits.

Kenina turned around glaring at her from several rows away, "Proof you don't belong here."

Dori stared right past her, ignoring her insults.

"Kenina, if you'd like to join us, the blackboard is at the front of the class," Professor Branton said as he waved his hand over the board writing the name of the class without touching the board, and aggressively underlining the word 'honors'. "You are all fourth year Sun students, and I expect the best from this class. You will also be mentoring a first year and midterms will be a collective project with your mentee," he continued.

Being the first day, each class was mostly just going through syllabi and getting textbooks. The first half of the day dragged on with Council History class following Sun honors, but the second half of the day was much more exciting. Dori headed to 'Concepts of Substance and Space' which was a Meta fairy class. Which also meant Kenina wouldn't be in this class, Dori had had to deal with her the entire first half of the day.

Professor Lenora greeted Dori with a smile as she walked into the classroom. "I was hoping to see you in this class, Endora. We've got quite the loaded syllabus," she said in her gentle, yet, authoritative voice as Dori walked through the door and took a seat front and center.

Professor Lenora stood tall and proud even in a simple classroom. Her long grey hair hung down to her hips, with intricate braids displayed throughout. She wore a vintage yellow floor length dress with little golden embossing and a long chain necklace with an amethyst stone hanging from it. One of the only amethyst stones Dori had ever remembered seeing. It was the rarest gem in all of Meltembra. Anonette Lenora was one of the most powerful Meta fairies ever known and had been asked several times to join the Council, practically being handed a position that many fairies spent years studying and lobbying for, but she had always denied. She always used the same excuse of loving to work with young fairies, helping the next generation of great fairies find their potential and what not. Dori never understood why she would want to spend time with teenage fairies, especially after 400 years, but Professor Lenora was her favorite teacher so she was glad she hadn't taken the council up on their offer, or retired.

"I wouldn't pass up an opportunity to be in one of your classes," Dori replied smiling back. "I have class with you every day of the week this year actually!"

"Good. You've got quite the year ahead of you. Did you hear my TA position opened up again?"

"Wait, really?" Dori replied excitedly.

"Apparently her schedule got too busy, and as runner-up if you are still interested—"

She didn't even have to finish the question before Dori answered. "Yes absolutely! I would be honored!"

Professor Lenora gave her a gentle smile, her face radiating peace and nobility. Her golden hazel eyes staring deep into Dori's soul. "Wonderful. See me after class and I will give you more details."

There was no hiding the smile Dori had plastered on her face. She opened her notebook and got ready for class to start as the rest of the students began arriving and taking their seats. She knew today would turn around.

CHAPTER 6

Mae had been waiting for Friday to arrive, since school had started this week Dori wasn't able to make any plans. They had spent nearly every day together for the two weeks before Dori started school. Mae was happy they had met towards the end of summer because Dori only asked once if she wanted to hang at the beach. She would've loved to but obviously couldn't. Mae had lied and said she wasn't a beach person, when in reality she would do anything to be able to walk on the warm sand in the daylight again.

She spent her days helping a new vampire move into the neighborhood. The poor thing hadn't been able to move with much, but Mae was able to show her the tunnels so she could get around during the day and the shops that welcomed their kind, as well as the ones that stayed open after nightfall. She was the first new vampire in decades, and had brought a daughter along with. Her daughter wasn't the only child in the village, the witches that lived there had relatively normal lives. They weren't immortal like the vampires so they lived full lives; they traveled on and off the island, got married, had kids, and died. They just lived with magic. There weren't too many kids, but the young girl wouldn't have to work hard to make friends, and wouldn't have to hide the fact her mom was a vampire. Even if most of the other kids were learning how to use magic and she was simply human.

Mae was glad she was merely in-charge of the newcomer and not her offspring as well. Mae was not a kid person, but their presence on the east side of the island made the village feel more normal. She could almost forget how much of a prison it was for her. She worked as a waitress at the local dinner, but never made enough to be able to get out of her house. She considered going to another part of the island and working nights, or maybe working at Conrad's coffee shop with the tinted windows, but her father or mother always claimed her time for some task or another. She would never be able to keep a job on any other part of the island, not that she could really get one since anyone who hired a vampire would be seen as a sympathizer and the fairies wouldn't have that.

No use worrying about all that now though, she was off to see her friend that she could be herself with. Well, other than the fact Dori still didn't know she was a vampire. Mae shrugged off that tiny detail. Since Dori was in school and had some school work to work on they were meeting at a library in the south, Mae had gotten there early through the tunnels and spent some time exploring the different book options. She simply told Dori she didn't have any homework yet, since Dori thought Mae had also started school this week, after all, she was technically still 17. Dori wondered what it must be like attending the little school on Delmira Island. She heard last year's graduating class size was about 70 students, whereas Zalor was double that.

Dori entered the library and went straight toward the back lounge area with bean bag chairs and fluffy rugs lining the floor. It smelled of old books and a hint of raspberry for whatever reason. Dori didn't know why it always smelled like that but she liked it.

Mae was already slouched back in a giant grey bean bag chair with a book in her hands, "Hey! How was the first week of classes?" Mae asked.

"It was alright, remember when I said my dad changed my schedule?" Dori asked as she sat in the bean bag chair right next to her friend. "Well, the classes he gave me are pretty boring, but I do have some really fun electives."

"At least you have those," Mae said encouraging her friend.

"Yeah, the other classes made the week kinda drag on, especially since this awful girl Kenina is in every single one of them," Dori said rolling her eyes.

Mae chuckled a little, "What's her issue?"

"Not 100 percent sure. A long time ago I got a silly award over her and she's had a chip on her shoulder ever since. Didn't help that her dad was up for a position that my dad ended up getting instead. She always used to pick on me when we were little about how her dad deserved the promotion and the privileges it came with more than my dad. And she's been extra mean to me ever since, doing everything she can to make my life in school miserable," Dori explained.

"That's a really weird thing for a kid to get worked up over," Mae commented.

"Well, my dad works in politics, I guess you could say, and he's got a really high level job now, so it kinda comes with status, which is just really fun," Dori said sarcastically. "And Kenina likes the spotlight but I got it. High school made it worse too," Dori paused rethinking the awful beginning of freshman year.

Mae waited for her to continue, she glanced to the side and back at her friend raising her eyebrow.

Dori decided to just dive into the story even though she did her best to forget it. "This guy I dated the beginning of freshman year, he was a new kid and a lot of girls were interested in him, I had met him a couple summers earlier and when he realized we were now at the same school he set his sights on me and ignored all those other girls. Worst of all, Kenina. She started some awful rumors about me and did all she could to break us up. It was a crappy relationship anyways so I didn't understand all the fuss over him," Dori looked down in shame and tried to shrug it off and opened her backpack to grab her homework.

"Ew, girls like that are the worst," Mae said, and felt a pang of empathy for her friend as she saw the look of shame on her face. "Do you want me to kill her?"

Dori looked up at her friend and laughed thinking she was joking, and briefly wondered if she was being serious. If Mae was a lost fae or of dark magic then she could genuinely be offering to kill her school bully.

Her train of thought was interrupted when someone called from amidst the book stacks, "Dori?" A head topped with blue hair popped around the corner and Sprig walked through the stack

"Hey, Sprig," Dori said.

"I thought I heard your laugh," Sprig said, smiling at her before he looked at the other girl in the lounge corner. "Who's your friend?"

"Oh, Sprig, this is Mae," Dori said gesturing in her direction, "Mae, this is Sprig. He lives down the road from me and makes a mean cup of coffee." Sprig's smile widened at the compliment.

"Nice to meet you," Mae offered with a smile and a gentle nod, eyes flickering from the handsome young man to her friend.

"Nice to meet you too," Sprig replied. "Sorry I can't stay and chat," he added turning to Dori. "Just had to grab a book that my little sister recommended for me. You're coming by the café tomorrow to try our new menu items right?"

"Yeah, of course!" Dori said excitedly.

"Okay great! See you then," Sprig said with a smile. "It was nice meeting you, Mae," he added, giving a small wave and walking back through the book stacks.

Dori smiled, turning back to her book, but noticed Mae staring at her from the corner of her eye. "What?"

"What do you mean 'What'? He is so into you! And he's cute!" Mae said nudging her friend's bean bag chair with her elbow.

"He is not into me, he's just really sweet. We're just friends! Have been for years." Dori said trying to turn back to her book.

"The way he smiled at you was *not* a 'just friends' smile," Mae watched her friend's cheeks turn red as she kept her eyes strained on the book in front of her. "Ah! And you so like him too!"

"What? No, I don't," Dori said defensively with a quick glance to look at Mae. "Plus, I'm with Abigor."

Mae abruptly turned around to completely face Dori. "Who?"

Dori pinched her lips together, "Oh, have I not mentioned him before?"

"NO!" Mae said nearly yelling, and a 'shh' came from another part of the library.

"Yeah, ummm, Abigor is my boyfriend. Of almost 3 years actually."

"We have known each other for weeks now, seeing each other almost every day, talking for hours, and you never mentioned having a boyfriend!" Mae said appalled. Then as she thought about it she continued. "So what's wrong with him?" She questioned, peering at Dori.

Dori chuckled, "What do you mean?"

"There has to be an issue if you haven't brought him up," Mae said. "Of all our talks, we've talked about your parents, your brothers, school, your favorite professor, and I even know your favorite book and how you like your coffee, almost no coffee with lots of cream and sugar," Mae remarked giving her friend a playful nudge. "Spill," she demanded.

"Well," Dori paused, "I feel distant from him lately, I mean last time I saw him was the day we met actually. He left the next day for a trip for work," she said attempting to keep it vague. She couldn't exactly mention he was on a Night fairy mission. "Everyone around us acts like we are the perfect couple, but I always feel like I need to fight for his attention, plus—" Dori stopped short trying to find the right words to explain it. "You know how I'm kinda weird?" Dori asked.

Mae smiled, "I would say really weird," she said thinking about the faces she makes while reading, and the way she gets excited about food, or the way she dances awkwardly across a room when she's in a good mood, instead of walking, "But go on."

"Well, even though we have similar personalities I feel like he doesn't like when I'm a major weirdo, and sometimes gets embarrassed by me, yah know?" Dori sighed.

"That's dumb," Mae responded bluntly. "So you feel like you don't get to be yourself around him?"

"Not always, especially not recently. Although the little bit of time away was kinda nice, and I do miss him," Dori said hopeful of his return. "And he's been sending sweet texts about how much he's missed me so maybe that's just what we needed."

"Well, I think you should be allowed to be yourself," Mae responded. "Maybe you should date Conrad," she said poking fun. "He always laughs when you dance across the coffee shop with your morning donut."

Dori laughed. "Yeah, except I'm pretty sure he likes you, so that wouldn't really work."

Mae laughed and they both turned back to their books shaking their heads. Dori's heart tugged in her chest and the war of her thoughts began again in her head. She loved Abigor. But - maybe that love had faded, he felt distant lately, like he was pulling away. The more Dori poured into herself the further she felt from Abigor. It was almost like she could either be happy or make him happy. Her face sank and she turned a little further in her bean bag chair so Mae wouldn't notice. Sprig was wonderful, but she had invested so much into her relationship with Abigor, their families welcomed each other in, he had been by her side through so much, even at their young age they had a life together, even if she kept this new life of hers from him. How could she possibly start over and give all that up? She shook the thoughts from her mind and attempted to remind herself that things would get better.

95

CHAPTER 7

The Night fairies would be arriving through the tower within Elandvor. Dori had allowed her father to give her a personalized tour of the intricacies of the tower since she would be waiting for Abigor's arrival later that day. She had been to the castle plenty of times but she always enjoyed touring the different rooms and seeing the magnificent architecture. Plus, her dad was elated to be able to show her around under "official business" this time since she was in her graduating year and could be a potential intern.

Their tour had been cut a little short when Cyrus was called away on urgent business. Dori wandered the halls looking at the intricate floor to ceiling stained glass windows, the fairy figures carved into the archways and the floral vines hanging from them. She knew she had entered the Dryad wing of the castle when the next hallway was covered in climbing ivy with the ceiling completely concealed in flowers and leaves. Large wooden chandeliers hung every few feet, casting a soft amber light in the space. She closed her eyes and breathed in the freshness of the air. Summer was indeed coming to an end, as the leaves were just beginning to turn colors and had the slightest feel of autumn magic. Dori was reminded that the holidays were right around the corner and got excited for all the merriment that was in her future. It was her favorite time of year. She felt a surge of energy; she loved the way nature made her feel.

She looked to her left through the open archways as a cool breeze came through. In the courtyard, a large fountain pool rippled in the breeze. Dori walked down the two little steps onto the pathway that went around the pool and watched the water spray in entrancing arcs. She walked up some steps which led to the upper part of the pool; the breeze causing the mist from the fountain to run down them in small rivulets. No one was around so all she could hear was the water moving and her own footsteps.

But her moment of peace ended as she heard some commotion coming from the tower behind her. The

Night fairies must be back from the trip. She was eager and flitted into sprite form to fly toward the base of the tower so she could meet Abigor as he returned. She flew over the Dryad wing of the castle she had been on the outskirts of, passed the Flora wing, and straight over the Meta wing, pausing for a moment as she gazed upon the glow of the architecture. Meta fairies have spacial magic, magic to create dimensions. Individually they usually could not manage enough power to create dimensions, but a group was powerful enough to create barriers between worlds, like the one that separated the human world and the fae world. Dori made it a point to come back and visit this part of the castle before she would be forced to choose her faction at the end of the year. She wanted to know all she could about her type of fairy before she officially declared it hers.

The Night wing of the castle was the furthest back and hugged the base of the tower. Since Night fairies are the protectors of the realm there was a small collection of elites who lived in the castle along side those in the council to ward off anything that may come for the tower. The tower was the pinnacle of the fairy world. Not only is it where the council meets but it housed portals to every major city in Meltembra. The top of the tower looked as though it was a circle of windows, but they were each a portal to the major cities of the factions around the world. One day, Dori hoped to be able to travel through the North Pole portal during Christmas time and see the Snow fairies in peak season.

As she looked up at the tower, the Shadowhead portal was still glowing brighter than the others after all that had traveled through. She flit down and landed in human form on the pressed stone walkway leading up to the winding staircases descending the tower and the elevators in between. There were lovers and families hugging one another at the return of the warriors. Dori thought emotions were a bit high for the occasion, the warriors had only gone to discuss progress on the war and recruit new fairies to come to Zalor and aid in protecting the city. Some families were in tears as if they had been off risking their lives, Dori became slightly concerned at what had happened while they were away that caused so much extra emotion.

As soon as she caught sight of Abigor in the crowd, she hurried over to him. Abigor dropped his bags and held her tight in his muscular arms. After twirling her around, he gently placed her back on the ground and gave her a soft kiss.

He pulled his lips away from hers and before opening his eyes he exhaled and whispered, "I missed you."

Dori smiled, touching the sides of his face, "I missed you, too," she said looking deep into his dark brown eyes. His gentle touch was exactly what she needed to calm the war in her head.

They walked off and Abigor told her about his trip; visiting the Takidaisu coast, dealing with the Selkie issue happening at the barrier into Japan, meeting new recruits and leading an informational assembly for prospective warrior fairies. He was glowing, figuratively, but Dori saw the glow as if it was literal, he seemed truly happy. She listened to him talk as they walked away from Elandvor back to his house. After greeting his family and leaving his bags behind, Abigor retrieved an item from one of them and headed back outside. He then guided Dori through the path near his neighborhood and towards the waterfalls located in the north beyond the city.

Hand in hand, they strolled through the Whispering Forest while discussing Abigor's journey and Dori's start to senior year. It felt like old times, the feeling of safety and passion as his fingers sat intertwined with hers. A pang of guilt pierced her heart. Had she merely been selfish in wanting more of his attention, he was pursuing his dream and she was here doubting him. Doubting her feelings for him, after years of ups and downs. Dori fought the rising anxiety in her as the bad memories threatened to flood over the joy in the moment. She reminded herself how good it felt to feel wanted by Abigor again and cleared her mind focusing on something else.

"Oh! And I made a new friend," Dori exclaimed.

"In your class?" Abigor questioned, it would be odd to have someone transfer in senior year at the most elite high school in the realm.

"No, I met her on the island. I ran into her one morning, actually, the day you left," Dori said.

"Oh, she's human," Abigor stated, giving a slight chuckle. "You Gregarious fairies and your humans," he said rolling his eyes jokingly and giving her a little nudge.

Dori knew Mae was some form of magical being, but she still wasn't quite sure what that was, and Abigor being a well-trained Night fairy would be paranoid at the mystery so she decided to keep that small detail to herself.

"Well, we have a lot in common and she's really nice! We have been spending a lot of time together," Dori continued thinking about the past two weeks with her new friend.

"Just be careful the amount of time you spend with her, and what you share," Abigor uttered with caution.

"I know I know," Dori said.

On the one hand Dori agreed with him, if Mae was a Banshee or some other type of lost fae, Dori could be in a lot of trouble for spending time with her. Dori believed it was unfair to generalize that all lost fae were evil, not all choose to live in the darkness, but were born into it, not that there were many left. Regardless, she felt that condemning an entire species was unjust.

On the other hand, Abigor thought Mae was human and still cautioned her against the friendship. Abigor, being a Night fairy, was Solidarity; Dori, leaning toward the Meta faction was Gregarious. Dori would make both Abigor and her father real happy by joining Sun and spending her days inside Meltembra, and stop associating with non-fairies.

As they approached the waterfall, Dori and Abigor took a seat at the edge of the lagoon on a large blue-gray boulder. Abigor took the small box out of his pocket and held it up to Dori. There was a catch in her throat and her lung, felt like blocks of ice. She didn't have time to think of what she would say if the box contained a ring and just hoped it didn't.

"I found this while I was away and thought it would be perfect for you," Abigor said as he opened the box.

Dori's lungs filled with with air again as she saw the necklace chain. She took a second to calm herself while she admired the pendent. It was a golden sun with wavy rays and a small fairy with gem wings sitting in the middle of it like the sun was a swing.

"Wow, it's gorgeous," Dori said.

"For a gorgeous woman," Abigor replied. "May I?" He asked lifting the necklace out of its box.

Dori grabbed her blonde locks in her hand and turned facing her back toward Abigor.

Undoing the clasp of the necklace he gently placed it around her neck, laying it softly on her sternum and clasping it again. He pulled his hands down her back as she let her hair fall again, touching the pendant.

"Thank you," Dori said looking over her shoulder at him.

He pulled her body closer to his and wrapped his arms around her, "You're welcome," Abigor said as he kissed the top of her head.

She leaned into him and they sat there on the side of the lagoon watching the water run down the falls. Dori breathed in the smell of sandalwood and leather from the strong man with his arms wrapped around her. A sense of peace settled on her heart; her mind was quiet for the first time in months. She reveled in the moment as her mind was at ease, and she believed that they could start anew and improve their relationship.

CHAPTER 8

In the following weeks, Dori's routine remained unchanged as she continued to spend her free time with Mae or Abigor. Waking extra early each morning before school to meet Mae, the pair would spend time in the library together working on homework. Despite his busy schedule with new recruits, Abigor continually made an effort to make time for Dori. He took her out on dates and leisurely strolls along the beach or through the forest. Her relationship with him continued to develop smoothly, and her bond with Mae grew stronger with each passing day. With her home life being so quiet, Jareth had been quite the hermit in his room, Dori felt like she was floating. As the season of Autumn unveiled its charms, the island shimmered with a vibrant cloak of oranges and reds.

Dori loved this time of year, as the holiday season approached the Dryad fairies prepared the foliage and the upcoming events, while the Tempes fairies began to bring in the change of weather. Since Delmira Island was located more north than other tropical islands, its residents experienced all four seasons. Located far east in the Atlantic, the closest locations were Nova Scotia and Bermuda, or you could take a straight shot west, into the US, but that would lead you to New Jersey and who would want to go there?

Most of the tourists visiting came through on cruises, as the Zalor Auroras were one of the marvels of the world. At least the human world. Delmira Island used to be a gateway between the human world and Meltembra. Fairy history says that when the worlds were divided, the city was enshrined in a mountain range, which still stands today. While the Northern Lights are typically seen only during the winter solstice, Delmira Island is blessed with the magical power of the city beneath it, which produces a year-round Aurora Borealis. The scientific explanation of this phenomenon may not convince everyone; saying it wasn't auroras at all but rather Strong Thermal Emission Velocity Enhancement (STEVE) caused by high-speed particle flow in the ionosphere, providing the purple ribbons in the sky above the mountains. No matter what visitors attribute the reasoning behind them; as long as the sky is clear, the island's visitors are treated to a breath-taking display of lights dancing across the sky almost every night. In the summer, when tourists flock to the island, the Tempes fairies ensure that the clouds stay away, leaving visitors in awe and eager to return.

With less tourism during the autumn season, the island became quieter with maybe one cruise a month. As a result, the fairies had more freedom to roam the island with fewer humans present. The island's locals were no strangers to the supernatural. Fairies and vampires were welcomed by most, as long as they followed certain etiquette. No flying or biting in public, and absolutely no discussions about the inter-species conflict. Behave appropriately in front of the locals, or you were not welcome.

The Harvest Festival was coming up and Dori decided to sit down at her sewing machine for the first time in months, to create something whimsical to wear. Dori wished she had the freedom to work with the Dryad fairies at this time of year; there was a sect of the faction called Harvest fairies, who changed the trees and plant-life to autumn colors and collected the harvest for yearly celebrations. Although, she did enjoy the role the Meta fairies had when it came to holidays. Nicknamed "Spirit fairies", they were always the hosts of the events, putting on the most fabulous parties. If the city was in good spirits, then the magic flowed brighter and fuller. The Harvest Festival was the start of months of celebration after celebration, truly the most magical time of year, and this year Dori genuinely felt hopeful that she could enjoy each celebration and be a part of the magic.

Dori felt alive again, motivation flowing through her. Her hands glowed with the magic of creating as she guided the fabric through the machine. Still working on her abilities, she created a simple dress that hung down like a handkerchief. As she worked on her magic, she discovered the ability to change the color of fabrics and changed the gentle yellow fabric that was leftover from summer into a dark rust-like orange. Sun fairies had the ability to control light, which, if powerful enough, meant the ability to change the perspective of things. Dori had practiced on a few fabrics before and had a hard time making the change stick, but she had changed this fabric a few days earlier and it had stuck so far. She was proud of herself and couldn't wait to wear her new creation to the festival next week.

As she hung her dress on a hanger and placed it in her closet there, was a commotion down stairs. She heard her mother shout her name and didn't hesitate to take up flight and zip down the stairs, her wings disappearing as soon as her feet hit the floor in the living room. Her mother and Jareth were helping an injured Abigor up the few steps from the front door. Dori's eyes were wide with panic.

"What happened?" She stammered as she reached to help.

Abigor looked up at her with tear-filled eyes, "Vampires," he said hoarsely.

Dori was terrified and frantically searched Abigor's body for any signs of punctures as the three of them placed him on the couch. A vampire bite was lethal to Night fairies; if he had been bitten he would be dead by morning and no amount of healing magic would help.

Abigor saw the terror in her eyes as she scanned his arms and neck, "No bites," he told her gently reaching up to her face.

Dori let out her breath in relief as she grabbed for her mother's hand and placed her other hand on Abigor's injuries.

"This is just proof something more needs to be done," Jareth said.

"Not now, Jareth," Adelyn said eyes still closed focusing her magic.

"It's never now!" Jareth began to shout, "These creatures are an abomination on our island! We need to be rid of the whole species!"

"Jareth, this war has been going on longer than either of us has been alive. We are trying to defeat the darkness but it's much easier said than done," Abigor stuttered. Dori hushed him and she moved down to Abigor's broken leg.

"This is going to hurt," she said to him. Adelyn and Dori both placed their hands on his broken bone using magic to reset and mend it. Abigor wailed. Night fairies had supernatural healing abilities, more than other fairies, but a break this bad would still take days to heal, that's why there were still teams of Meta fairies that worked with the warriors. Dori hated seeing him in pain, she pushed her emotions back best she could, ignoring the pit in her stomach. She continued to heal the scratches and bruises on her boyfriend, attempting to relieve as much pain as she could.

Of course Jareth wasn't able to suppress his feelings ever. Each hand went ablaze and he started babbling about how vampires were a disease and witches needed to be held responsible for the deaths they caused by creating such creatures.

Dori snapped her head around, "You are not helping!" she said, practically biting Jareth's head off. "Why don't you grab some towels and cleaning supplies so we can clean the blood off the couch when we are done!" Dori roared.

"You stupid spirit fairies are so emotional! You're not willing to do what's necessary to create a better world," Jareth said storming off.

"Endora," Abigor said reaching his hand to her face, she grabbed his hand in hers, meeting his gaze. "I'm sorry."

"What are you sorry for?" She asked.

But he was fading, the pain and healing magic took a lot out of him and she didn't want to keep him up. She placed a hand on his head and helped him into sleep, hoping she was still strong enough to give him peaceful dreams.

114

CHAPTER 9

Dori was thankful to see Mae's text the following morning so she could confide in her friend, even if it was extra early. She waited on the dock in the southeast of the island, they had spent a lot of time around here after some late nights in the library just a few blocks away. The boardwalk on the south of the island was practically abandoned in the off-season, it was a quiet, peaceful place the friends loved spending time at. Mae walked across the gloomy hill and grabbed Dori's arm from behind, turning her around.

Dori knew something was wrong the instant she spun around, but instead of asking she just stared at her friend, waiting.

Mae took a deep breath and looked into Dori's eyes, "I have to tell you something, and I think you have something to tell me too."

Dori froze. She let out a breath gazing to the side and paused. Finally she looked up at Mae and said, "Okay, let's both say our secret at the same time."

Mae nodded in agreement. Dori held up three fingers and held her breath as she slowly put one at a time down.

Dori spoke in a frantic terrified tone as she spat out her secret as Mae closed her eyes and spoke at a calm almost whisper as she said hers.

"I'm a fairy."

"I'm a vampire."

Mae opened her eyes and looked at Dori as if she were the most dense creature on the planet, "Of course you are a fairy!" she yelled "Would you like to elaborate on that?" She sassed.

Dori was too confused by her friends initial statement to focus on her question. "You're really a vampire?" She recalled back to when they first met, on the east of the island. How could she have been so foolish? But she couldn't stop thinking about the light she could sense in Mae's aura. Dori's head was rambling on, and she began to ramble out loud. "I mean I guess that makes more sense since I don't ever recall any Banshees around here."

Mae's head jerked back, "Banshees?"

"Yes. I knew you were a magical creature but I wasn't sure what kind. You aren't from our realm, so I thought you were one of the lost fairy kin. I didn't think you were of witch magic though."

Mae looked at her and shook her head, "We will come back to the lost kin thing later. You knew?"

"Well yeah. Fairies detect magic in the human world. But your magic has light that's why I didn't think you were of witch magic"

"What does that even mean?"

"Fairies and witches have opposite types of magic. Fairy magic is natural and *mostly* meant to produce good, whereas witch magic is *artificial*," she said using air quotes. "Produced in dark practice and, more often than not, produces evil," Dori paused and looked at her friend, "No offense."

"Okay, we can come back to all that later. Yes, I am a vampire, meant for evil," she hissed as she gave a sly smirk. "But I still need to know who you are."

Dori had completely forgotten about Mae's earlier question. "Right, sorry. My full name is Endora Nova Teresi, born of the Sun and Meta factions."

"And the not-so-great boyfriend of yours?"

"Abigor Luan, of the Night Warriors Faction. What about him?"

"Oh, well he and my brother had a nice little chat yesterday, while he was heaving wooden daggers into half a dozen vampires."

Dori's eyes grew wide, "Your brother was one of the ones he fought last night?"

"You knew about it?" Mae asked in surprise.

"Well, yeah. He came to my house after so we could heal his injuries, Night fairies do heal faster than normal but his injuries were bad. The group of vampires they were protecting us from must've been vicious." Dori began to wonder, Abigor hadn't mentioned being on duty last night; so why was he out fighting? Dori hadn't gotten to ask Abigor anything about last night.

Mae scoffed, "A damn princess protected by monsters who call themselves warriors."

Dori snapped back. "First of all. I am no princess. Fairies do not have royal families anymore, no kings or

queens. We have leaders who help guide our people."
She let her anger show ever so slightly as she hissed
her next words, "and the warriors may be cruel at
times but they protect our people *and* the humans.
Vampires are the *savages* that live off blood!" Just as
the hurtful word slipped through her lips she realized
the gravity of what she had just said.

"SAVAGES?!" Mae screeched. "Your pompous little
boyfriend followed my brother near the east side
of the island, leading a group of drunken fairies to
attack the vampires *unprovoked*." She let that last
word lay heavy in the air as she just stared at her
friend.

Dori paused. She looked down, "I didn't mean it
that way. All I have ever known is that vampires are
hostile. We have been at war for the centuries since
they came—"

Suddenly Mae turned around and put a hand up
behind her to quiet Dori. She listened in close and
heard foot steps in the distance.

"Someone's coming" she whispered, turning
around staring Dori in the eyes "turn into your fairy
form and hide."

Dori did as she was told, quickly shifting into her natural state and flitting under the dock. She peaked around the wooden post and watched an older man appear next to Mae from the woods, who definitely gave off vampire energy. They spoke for a moment, and then a soft glow appeared beneath her feet as both vampires looked to the sun breaking over the horizon and disappeared in a flash. Frantic, Dori looked side to side but there was no sign of either of them. Her phone gave a small buzz and she pulled it out of her pocket.

New Message from Mae

Wait another 5 minutes, then meet me at the library. The higher the sun the safer you are.

She turned around to see the sun cresting over the horizon. The grey of night faded as the oranges and reds flashed their lines across the ocean. Dori loved this sight. Normally this view would lift her spirits in an instant, but she felt she had wronged her friend, been too harsh. She contemplated all that had been said as she watched the sun come up for those few minutes. The Sun fairy in her jolted back absorbing the magic of the moment. It was a rush that she normally experienced in human form when sitting on the beach, but her fairy glow now mimicked the sky before her. She shined even brighter with oranges, reds, and pinks all while keeping her usual purple hue. She closed her eyes and reveled in the moment as her hair blew back in the wind.

Taking a deep breath she opened her eyes again and looked from side to side. There was no one but her. Dori flitted out toward the sand and turned back into her human form. She quickly removed her sandals and spread her toes in the warming sand. The feeling brought a smile to her face, but she reminded herself she had somewhere to be. She started toward the library, sandals in hand.

Just as Dori arrived to the library, she saw her friend scurrying about in the back corner of the library. Mae had collected a handful of books on each of their species; *Fairy Folklore, Fairies in the Real World, Vampires Real or Not Real, Truth Bites, Myths and Realities of Vampires,* etc. Dori looked confused as she reached the table, Mae stacked one more book on top of her pile proudly and a little more loudly that she ought to have been in a library, misting dust in each direction.

"Okay, here's what we are going to do. You and I both have plenty of questions, let's start with the truth about our species, then we can get into the details we have been hiding as we have gotten to know each other these last few weeks," Mae stated proudly.

Dori nodded, her friend was obviously in problem-solver mode. Though frustrated about the events of last night, Dori was curious and did have many questions, so she agreed. "Sounds great, who goes first?"

"I will," Mae replied. "I think fairy history is much longer and confusing, so I'll just get mine over with before we get into all that." They both gave a sly smile, and Dori's cheeks turned pink.

Mae began. "It's quite simple. As you know vampires were created by witches as a survival mechanism, a search for power; what they didn't know is you can either be witch or vampire, so they lost their magic abilities but gained new vampire powers. The normal ones you hear are the ones that are true, speed, heightened sense of smell and hearing, supernatural healing, and we can compel others." Mae rolled her eyes and continued, "No, we don't have a fear of garlic and holy water won't melt us. Weaknesses are sun and wooden stakes, as you know. Garlic and holy water are myth, however, cinnamon is like poison." Dori looked confused, as if never hearing that one before but didn't interrupt. Mae looked at her friend and decided to continue on with a more personal truth since it was related. "And yes," she regretted having to say the next words, "vampires are hunters. Predators. And *most* are malicious killers with no regrets, but many aim to live at peace among humans so they do not kill when they feed. We survive off blood, not death. So we make do with non-lethal feeding so we don't have police or fairies coming after us. Plus those that indulge in death more become the grotesque type of vampires that older folklore will show you. The darker your deeds, the more demon-like your appearance," Mae looked down taking a deep breath; she looked back up and said, "Your turn."

Dori started off with an apology, "Mae, I am sorry. I want you to know I have never felt threatened by you, even without knowing what you are. We got caught up in fighting someone else's fight and I'm sorry for how I responded earlier."

Mae gave a slight nod and pulled at her lips, "I am sorry too, but still need to understand more of what's going on. All you" she reminded gesturing to the fairy books.

Dori inhaled, "Alright, well first, it's easiest to understand history as far back as we can go. Humans and fairies used to coexist, but when some humans started to take advantage of fairies and even enslave them, fairies separated themselves and the Fae realm was made so only fairies could enter and they hid themselves from the humans. Many fairies held a grudge against the humans for the pain that was caused and giving up this world; feeling as though we shouldn't have run and be forced to live in hiding, especially as the stronger species. Those factions split in many directions, some pursued unnatural magic to increase their power, becoming witches—"

"Wait, witches were once fairies?" Mae interrupted in surprise.

"Well, yeah. Just about all magic originates in fairy magic. There can either be natural magical beings or unnatural. Like, Mermaids, they were once a sect of Water fairies that were cursed to never be able to leave the water. Phoenixes emerged from a charm created by Sun and Fauna magic." Dori paused letting her friend absorb all she was saying. She continued in a gentle tone, "Witches were born of a group of radicals, made up of many fairy tribes with one goal in common. Revenge on humans. But their sacrificial magic led to their banishment from the Fae realm. I guess kind of like how you can be either witch or vampire." Dori shrugged continuing, "A fairy's magic thrives on life, and witch magic is fueled by death. At least it was, there are more natural ways of practicing witchcraft nowadays, but the original witches created a divide between magics, and a good amount of witches hate both humans and fairies for that." Mae nodded as if signaling her friend to continue.

"The Fae realm is essentially a copy of earth, but it looks a little different. Like this island for example, we have some shops along the beachfront just like here, but the mountains in the middle of the island is actually the largest city in our world. This island is just a quiet little vacation spot here on earth but in our realm, it's a hub for all fairies coming and going, kind of like New York City or Dubai. But instead of buildings and minimal nature, the buildings are built into nature, and we have a tower with portals that lead to other major cities around the world, our own Grand Central." Dori paused realizing she was getting slightly off track. "Anyways, fairies have done everything to try and weed out any weakness, which is where we get the different factions.

"Fairies realized there was more strength, really less weakness, with only harnessing one type of magic, and fairies were less vulnerable to dark magic, so they decreed each fairy must choose a primary magic and is able to choose a secondary type to help aid in their first." Mae looked at her friend with a puzzled gaze. Dori smirked and continued, "Essentially if you are born from a Sun fairy line you will most likely stay a Sun fairy. It's rare for a fairy to choose a power they were not born with, mainly because it is harder to learn a magic you are not raised in. Which is partially why the island exists. It is full of every faction, and a school that teaches each type of magic. It's a place where all fairies come together, which is why the leaders on the island are so critical."

"And that's where your family comes in right?" Mae offered.

"Yes, my grandfather was one of the great leaders of the city for many years and my dad stepped into his role about 50 years ago. And which is why since Abigor is from another faction, and has potential to be one of the city's leaders, when he and I started dating the council within the city decided it was a match and proclaimed us betrothed. Something about fate and the spirits bringing us together for the good of the city," Dori said, trying not to sound salty.

Mae's jaw dropped, "Wait so this wasn't even like an arranged marriage planned at your birth, you started dating this guy and your people decided it was forever?"

"Pretty much," Dori huffed, allowing the sad dazed look to drop in her eyes.

"Oh my god. You hate it!" Mae gathered.

Dori shook the expression from her face and began to defend her relationship, "No, no!... I mean it was great long ago, I fell for him so fast. But, as I've gotten older I've just, realized our personality's don't match as much as I thought they did and I just...kind of feel..."

"Trapped," Mae finished her thought for her.

Dori just looked up at her friend with a blank expression. Mae knew the answer. They sat in silence for a moment and Mae decided it best to come back to that. Mae grabbed a book and flipped through quickly.

"Okay but if this island is so important why isn't it in any of these books?"

Dori smiled, "because this is fairy folklore," she waved a book around in her hand sarcastically. "We are talking reality here." Both girls gave a small laugh.

"Plus, it's safer if the location of the biggest fairy city in the world is just talked about in legend. The books are close to accurate on the different types of fairies though. 7 types overall, split into 3 gregarious and 4 solidarity." Dori was happy to be back on the less personal topics. "Gregarious often live here in human form and travel to the Fae realm, whereas Solidarity live in the realm and rarely come out into the world other than when preforming their duties. They mostly stick to being in fairy form but gregarious like to stay in human form more often." Mae nodded with her bottom lip sticking out a bit, Dori could tell she was over the excess information dump.

"Okay, how about we switch gears and you can tell me more about your family?" Dori offered.

"Oh. Alright," Mae adjusted her position in her seat and gave a deep sigh "My parents were both into the supernatural, my mom was a witch and my dad a researcher. They came to this island to study why it's such a power surge, though my brothers and I thought we were coming here on vacation. Then my dad met Zagan—"

"Wait wait wait," Dori threw here hands up motioning Mae to stop, then slammed them down on the table in front of her. "Your dad met Zagan? Like, THE ZA-GAN? The leader of the vampires."

Mae began to nod but then tilted her head, "Wait, do you know him?"

"No, of course not! But for the past 300 years, or so I've heard, we have all learned about him and his reign of terror," Dori pulled back a grit her teeth. "Sorry, that's probably an insult."

Mae smirked "I mean you're not wrong. He's actually the reason my family became vampires." Dori's eyes got wide, but she stayed silent. Mae took that as note she ought to continue. "Zagan met my dad, an ego-maniac obsessed with power, well informed on the supernatural. So he turned him into a vampire."

That last sentence hung in the air a while but Mae knew the story didn't get any lighter so she just piled on.

"My father told my mother Zagan wanted them to stay on the island and for my father to be second in command. My mother was reluctant but as she thought it over my father made the decision for her. He knew she would've been beneficial to the community as a witch but he was not going to live through his immortal life without her, so he turned her."

"Wait... so you're saying—"

"Yes," Mae paused. "My father killed my mother." She looked off in the distance and continued to rip off the bandaids, "my brothers and I were young. My mother had another witch cast protective spells on us so we could be a little older before we turned and then one night they turned us all. They always said it was for our protection, there were too many supernatural out there that would want to hurt Zagan and our father so we needed to be un-killable," Mae took another breath. "That was 200 years ago."

"So when we said we were pretty much the same age..." Dori just grinned at her friend in an attempt to lighten the mood. It worked.

Mae smiled wide, biting the tip of her tongue in between her perfectly white teeth. "Yes Dori. We are the same age, but I've been 17 for 200 years," she sneered and shook her head. They looked at each other for a moment then both burst out laughing. As they remembered they were in the library they started shushing each other and it made them each laugh harder. Then Dori was taken aback by a familiar voice.

"Dori, are you in here?"

Dori shushed her friend as Mae mouthed the words *who is it*. Though she swore she said them out loud. She tried again and realized she was speaking but no words were coming out, Dori waved her hand a a brief glimmer of light sparkled between her fingers. Then Mae was gone. Mae looked from side to side and saw everything through a shiny stained glass type lens. She was still sitting across from Dori but she had a feeling no one could see her. She saw this pretentious, dark-haired, young man walking through the library stacks in Dori's direction.

"Abigor! Hey," Dori said while turning around in her seat to face him.

You've got to be kidding me. Mae attempted to say but apparently she was still mute. Which just made her angry. That and the fact he looked perfectly fine after the ordeal from last night, Dori did mention healing him.

"Hey sweetheart," Abigor said as he kissed Dori on the forehead and took a seat next to her.

Mae felt nauseous. Which is saying something since vampires don't get sick. This was nausea of pure disgust.

"What are you doing here?" Dori said as she quickly glanced to the side to verify her invisibility enchantment was still holding up okay. She turned back to Abigor with an innocent smile.

"Looking for you," he expressed as he jumped up grabbing her hands. "Let's go to brunch," he began to pull her up out of her seat. Just as she began to involuntarily lift off the seat she pulled back on his hands and forced herself back down. Mae mocked his words with as much disgust as she possibly could on her face, not that anyone could see.

"You seem to be in a good mood," Dori said thinking about the events of the previous night. "And actually I was kind of in the middle of something." As she said it she realized the books behind her would probably be a really odd thing for him to discover and began frantically trying to think of excuses. She wished she had other books to put on top of the open ones that were displayed on the table. She moved to the side a little to deter him from seeing them behind her and added, "can I meet you in a couple hours?" with a coy smile.

Abigor looked anyway. "Sweetheart," he said densely, "I think you've studied your metaphysics and human history enough for midterms. I wanted to bring you out and thank you for last night."

Dori looked behind her and saw the books Abigor had just described. She was amazed at herself. She simply thought hard enough and her magic had expressed the desire. That sunrise this morning charged her magic more than she knew possible, especially after the exhaustion of last night. She looked back at her boyfriend and began to negotiate.

"You're probably right but let me just pack things up and I can meet you in an hour?" She swung his hands in hers.

"Good enough for me," Abigor said as he leaned down and kissed Dori on the forehead. "Meet me at The Boathouse at Ten."

"Ooooh, fancy," Dori remarked as she raised her eye-brows.

He began to walk away but turned back, looking Dori once over and added, "Yes, so change into something a little nicer?" He looked down towards her legs, "And a tad longer." That last part not being a suggestion.

Dori smiled slightly and acknowledged. She watched him walk away then turned around and released her friend from her bubble. Mae gasps as if needing air and Dori looked at her concerned.

"First of all, what in the *witchcraft* was that?"

Dori opened her mouth to respond but Mae kept going.

"And *THAT* is Abigor? The 'handsome' and 'brave' Night warrior?" She quoted with her fingers as her lip tore to one side in disgust. "Seriously?" She added and cocked her head toward her friend while throwing up her hands in utter confusion.

Dori was confused at that last part. "You don't think he's handsome?" Dori asked.

"Nooooo." Mae responded with no hesitation.

Dori threw her head back slightly with a wide smile releasing a breath with the echo of a laugh on it.

"What is funny?" Mae asked

Dori shrugged looking back over her shoulder at where Abigor had walked out and then back to her friend, "I think he's cute," then she defended her boyfriend ever so slightly "and he *is* brave, for the record. He's protected our people for many years and his community before that."

Mae just looked her friend straight in the face and said, "he's a putz."

Dori's jaw dropped. "You just saw him for the first time! You didn't even meet, and I've barely said anything about him."

"Dude, do I really need to explain," Mae leaned over the table inching closer to her friend looking at her befuddled. "Okay, first of all, the kiss on the forehead." Dori attempted to interrupt but Mae put her hand up right on her face. "And the way he said 'sweetheart' so..." she tried to find the right word to phrase it but just settled for a disgusted noise instead. "So blehhh. When he pointed out the books, which nice cover by the way." Mae nodded her approval not even looking at Dori.

Dori raised her hand to try and respond but Mae's hand had not moved from her mouth. Mae just continued.

"Oh my gods, but, the worst of all! The comment on your clothes!" Her aggression got the better of her and she started to squeeze Dori's face without realizing it. "What is wrong with your cute purple sundress?" She started to yell, "That's perfect for a date at the nicest restaurant in a beach town!" A handful of shushes came from different directions in the library and Mae relaxed a little as her face expressed the *oops* she felt.

Dori used this opportunity to peel Mae's hand from her mouth as she sarcastically muttered "ow."

Mae looked back at her friend and realized the clamp she had on her face. "My bad." She offered with a saddened smile.

"Okay, so lemme back track a second," Dori let Mae sit back in her seat as she began to close and stack all the books they had gathered. "Sun fairies can manipulate light, and light bounces off of everything and is how we see, so I am able to make myself, things, or others, appear invisible. And as a Meta fairy, we have dimensional powers, and since I didn't have time to explain and make sure you stayed still, I used those powers to create a bubble around you so you couldn't effect anything and give away that you were there." Dori let out a sigh, "As for Abigor, we will have to get to that later. We should get these books back, and I have to get changed."

Mae looked at her in question, "Are you really going to have time to go back to your house in the realm and change, come back to the shore and meet him in an hour? Forget what he said! What you're wearing is fine!" Mae demanded.

"Though I agree with you, and I love this dress, he gets weird about this stuff. And... remember how I just said I can manipulate dimensions?" Dori began to grin, "I don't have to go back home to get anything." She walked backwards with a stack of books in her hands proudly. Mae grabbed her own stack and followed her friend.

CHAPTER 10

After putting the books away the girls walked into the bathroom, after making sure no one else was in there Dori locked the door. She turned to Mae.

"Okay, now. Don't freak out," Dori said slowly.

Mae, having been alive for over two centuries and seen witches perform crazy spells, thought her friend was being a little dramatic. But then Dori's hands began to glow with yellow and purple; illuminating sparkles interwove between her fingers. Purple light lifted off her hands like flames, and coalasced into a swirling ball between them. She thrust the ball towards the wall on the opposite side of the room. Mae watched the light pass by her and followed it to the wall, where it burst and lit the wall from top to bottom in yellow light. Dori walked across the room and stood, back to the yellow wall, and smiled at Mae.

"What am I looking at?" Mae asked confused.

"My closet," Dori replied as she waved her hand over the wall making it transparent.

The wall had been transformed into a small closet, hanging clothes and a few drawers underneath just like any ordinary closet but with the same glassy glow as the bubble Mae was in just minutes before.

"It's not just an illusion?" Mae asked as she slowly approached the wall.

"See for yourself. Reach in and grab something," Dori directed her friend, stepping aside.

Mae was reluctant, but Dori gave her a reassuring nod and she reached her hand through the wall. She grabbed for the first thing her hand touched and out came a little blue summer dress on a hanger. Mae was amazed.

"I cast this enchantment a while back, my little brother knows about it, but no one else does. We aren't really supposed to use dimensional magic like this, it is technically for 'selfish motives' and that's a 'gateway to darkness'," Dori said, using air quotes and rolling her eyes. "But I work hard on some of my clothes and after Jareth lit our living room on fire and ruined our couches I didn't want something happening to my hard work.

Which worked out great because he's torched the whole house a few times and not everything is reversible with magic."

Mae look at her confused. "So this keeps your closet safe from fire? ... Wait so your brother's anger outbursts turn into legit fire?" Mae's jaw dropped and she looked frantically from side to side. "Like *actual* freaking fire?"

"Right, we haven't covered that yet," Dori said. "Yeah, my dad is a Sun fairy, so me and my brothers were all born with that power, and my brother struggles controlling his fire abilities because he can't control his temper," Dori said simply and gave a shrug.

Her friend gazed upon her with awe, marveling at her unflinching composure. Dori spoke as if this was normal but even for fairies, that can't be a healthy way to live. Mae didn't know what to say, she had so many questions but a limited amount of time before her friend had to leave. "Okay, so we have a lot to discuss. Can you meet me back here after your 'brunch' with Abigor," she said mockingly. "I am pretty much stuck here til sundown anyway."

"Yeah, sounds perfect," Dori said, shaking her head at her friend's mockery, trying to hide how much it actually hurt. She reached into her closet and pulled out the orange dress she had just finished making the day before and showed it to her friend. Mae looked the dress up and down and shrugged a bit, she was obviously still bitter about Dori having to change at all, and Dori tried not to be insulted by Mae's judgement on her recent creation. Abigor had this way about him, Dori had become used to following along, though she hadn't seen it in a while. Things had been going well, now, here listening to her friend's judgement, she was questioning her relationship again. She reached in and grabbed a long layered white skirt, "Maybe this with the jean jacket I was wearing?" she offered holding the skirt out to her side.

"Have anything darker?"

Dori pulled her lips together, lifted the skirt higher than her head and waved her hand in front of the skirt. Then with a quick pinch of the fabric it turned into an earthy brown color.

Mae looked at the skirt as her jaw fell open, "How did you—?" she questioned turning back to her friend.

"Just another trick I learned," Dori said. "Here try this on," she grabbed her light blue jean jacket she had been wearing earlier and turned it black as she handed it to her friend.

Mae couldn't help but smile. She grabbed the jacket and put it on as she faced the mirror. "Wow. This may be the coolest thing I've ever seen a fairy do."

Mae looked at the time, she turned back to the closet and shifted through a bit more, finally coming out with the velvety fall-orange top. "This, with some black pants, add a jacket and you're golden."

Dori stared at the top, "I haven't actually worn that before. I made it the first time Jareth lit the house on fire, and I could never bring myself to wear it again," she said gazing down at her hands as she anxiously wrung them together.

"You made this? It's stunning. And a little spicy," Mae said with a tone of glee.

Dori looked up at her with question.

Mae smirked, "Abigor wants you to wear something nice but 'longer'," she uttered, disgusted. "So, cute crop and—" she grabbed a pair of bell bottom pants, "Can you make these sparkly black?" She asked her friend with wonder in her eyes.

Dori looked at her and entertained the notion of actually showing up to her date in such a daring outfit, changing the pants as requested. Once a simple denim to a deep sparkling black. She looked at the outfit her friend held out to her hesitant.

"Endora," Mae said grabbing her friends attention. It was the first time Mae had used her full name and her eyes met Mae's as she stared into her soul. "You are beautiful and bold. No boy should ever tell you how to dress. If you are comfortable in this, rock it. Don't let your boyfriend or your brother dictate your life. You made this! You should show it off," Mae said earnestly.

Dori smiled with a tear beginning to well in her eye, but she grabbed the clothes from her friend and dared to be confident for once. She quickly changed in the stall and came out twirling showing off her outfit as she walked to the mirror to look at herself.

"Yes!" Mae shouted. "Get it!"

Dori turned around hugging her friend. "Thank you," she whispered.

"No, thank you for blessing me with your presence!" Mae said amusingly. "Now go show your stupid boyfriend how lucky he is to know you. And snag me a roll or two."

Dori walked back to the glowing wall and removed a backpack from her closet handing it to Mae.

"What's this?"

"Well, you're stuck here and all this library has is folklore, so here's my backpack with my current textbooks and notebooks in it. It'll give you a little glimpse into the fairy world," Dori told her. "Just don't mess up my homework, I have to hand that in."

Mae nodded. "Let's do this. See you in a few hours?"

Dori smiled and waved her hand to turn the wall back into the plain off-white it was before. "See you then."

The sun was bright and the air filled with the sweet smells of fall. Walking down the boardwalk, Dori felt a bit self-conscious about her outfit. However, as a few people complimented her along the way, her spirits lifted. By the time she got to the boathouse she was loving the feeling of confidence and eager to eat, she didn't care how Abigor reacted, she was happy. Though her joy slowly slipped away as soon as she saw him.

Still in the waiting area, Abigor stood to greet her. A flicker of a smile at the sight of her, then his face fell in judgement. "What are you wearing?" His eyes glared from her slightly exposed midriff to her face.

Dori held tight to her excitement. "I made this shirt a while back and finally decided to wear it," she said smiling at him. "Don't you like it?"

Before he could answer a woman leaving the restaurant squealed, "Girl, I love your outfit!"

"Thank you," Dori gleamed unable to hide her joy. She looked back at Abigor's blank face, then they were summoned as their table was ready.

Abigor remained silent as they were seated and the waitress took their drink orders. "I thought you were done with making clothes?" he asked as soon as she left.

"I haven't had much time to do it lately but I still love doing it," she said deciding to roll with the conversation. "Actually, I just made a new dress last night," she added proudly.

"Shouldn't you be focusing on your career? Not some hobby? You've only got so much time before declaring your faction and you haven't even decided what you want to do after high school," Abigor said slightly agitated.

"It's not a hobby, and it *is* what I want to do. I want to design clothes, maybe open up a shop here on the island or in Zalor, filled with my creations," Dori said, as her imagination ran wild with the thought of it. Then Mae's voice echoed in her head, 'putz' she had called him, and Dori definitely felt like that was true in this moment. She grit her teeth as the word hobby taunted her, thinking about Mae's ability to see Abigor's true colors from one instance.

"What about the council? What about the intern-ship?"

"What about it? You know I never wanted anything to do with the council. I don't even want to do the stupid internship."

"That internship is the start of the life we've been working towards, the door is open to you and you're just going to throw it away?" Abigor said insulted.

"What are you talking about, the life *we* have worked for?"

Before Abigor could answer the waiter came back, Dori picked up her menu and spent the entire time Abigor was ordering his food frantically deciding what to get while her anxieties ran wild in her head.

"Um, I'll just take a burger please, no tomato," Dori said when it was her turn to order. "And can I also add a Phoenix Fizz please," she asked handing her menu to the waiter, she heard Abigor scoff out a laugh. As soon as he walked away Dori's smile disappeared as her eyes met Abigor's. His jaw moved side to side as he held back his frustration, curling his lip with disdain, Dori jumped back to the conversation.

"You know I don't want to join the council, never have. Can we just try and have a nice meal? I don't really want to think about factions and careers right now," Dori said simply.

"I know that, but what about us? The life we plan to have, you'd rather run some shop then be a part of the most important thing in our culture?"

Some shop echoed fiercely in her mind enticing her fiery spirit. "What's wrong with following my dream?"

Abigor stared at her, "You're right. We can talk more about this another time."

Dori was happy to see the waiter approaching with her sparkling red beverage and watched Abigor's disapproving look as he sipped on his water. He hated spending excess money, this brunch alone was an extra special occasion, but he never ordered anything other than water from a restaurant, he thought it was a waste of money. Even for special occasions he would pressure her to order water and the cheapest thing on the menu. Dori was no fan of the beverage prices either and didn't mind just getting water usually, but she wanted to feel like she was allowed to order something more than the cheapest things on the menu when she wanted. This small act of defiance felt more than justified. She knew this date was to thank her for last night, so didn't she at least deserve a nice drink, especially when she couldn't even have decent conversation.

Per usual Abigor held the conversation, Dori pretended to not have much going on in life and stayed quiet to let him have the attention. It had been a while since he made her feel like this, things had been going so well. She decided to brush off the conversation, apparently her outfit stirred him in a really wrong way, one rough conversation shouldn't weigh her down this much, not after weeks of good times.

All the confidence that had bolstered in her before faded from Dori's spirit. Insecurities roared within her and she couldn't wait to get back to the library and change.

ℭHAPTER 11

Mae was rummaging through the fairy folklore books comparing bits of information to Dori's textbooks when her friend walked through the stacks to the back corner. She slumped down in the bean bag chair wrapping her jacket tightly around her. Mae looked at her and knew the date didn't go well.

"I'm gonna want to kill him even more, won't I?" Mae said glaring at her friend.

Even though Dori realized Mae wasn't joking, she smiled. The one person, well not a person, in the world who always had her back, and she'd only been in her life for a couple months. She was so thankful.

She told Mae about the date as they walked to the bathroom and Dori changed her clothes. Dori reassured her friend she would've wanted to change anyway; no point in being all dolled up to sit in a bean bag chair at the library.

"So what exactly does he expect of your life together? He goes off and fights the big bad vampires and comes home to his well-manicured politician wife?" Mae questioned aggressively.

"We didn't really get back to that, I don't know what he expects, he's always encouraged me to do the internship but never outright said that's what *he wants* me to do. I don't understand why my dreams bother him so much."

"Because he's small minded. Didn't you say your dad treats your creative side more as a hobby too?"

"Yeah, he wants something concrete so he knows I'm taken care of, art in any sense is a hard field to be in, whereas the council is eternal so I'm set for life, no matter how many lifetimes I live."

"Oh yeah so you're not immortal like me but you still live a long time right?" Mae asked pulling a book from her stack.

"Yeah, our aging slows when we turn 18, depending on how powerful you are 10 years around the sun is a year of aging. The more powerful you are the longer you tend to live."

"So if you live til 80, or so..."

"I would be about 600," Dori said. "Most fairies live somewhere between 600 and 800 years. Actually reaching that 10 is a super hard thing to do, so the aging is more like 8 years for average power fairies. I actually have a teacher who is 789, she's a really powerful meta fairy."

"Let me guess that's your favorite teacher you're the TA for, what was her name again?"

"Professor Lenora, and yeah she's really great, the class is actually Concepts of Substance and Space, a Meta fairy specialty. The space part of metaphysics is where the dimensional powers come from, like my closet trick and the portals to Meltembra."

"Interesting, so the council is like a government and each faction has a representative that's kinda like a president and they all work together to run the world, am I understanding that right?" Mae asked

"Well, yeah pretty much, I guess you got through a lot," Dori nodded in approval. "Each faction has a head, they're called Elders, and the Elders have a right hand, called an Adjudicate. That's my dad's position. He's been an Adjudicate for as long as I've been alive," Dori explained.

"So he's like a vice president of the Sun fairies?"

"In a way, yeah, I guess."

"And that's what he wants you to do? Work your way up to what, take his place?" Mae asked confused.

"I guess, except I would be primary Meta fairy so I would represent a different faction," Dori said thinking more about how trapped she felt.

"What do you mean *'would be'?*" Mae asked.

"Well, when you graduate high school you declare one faction, you can have a secondary type of magic but even that's been uncommon lately. You are told to focus your energy on one magic in order to prolong your life and become more powerful," Dori told her friend with the taste of disdain on her lips.

"Why do I get the feeling you hate everything you just said?"

"I do! It doesn't make any sense!" Dori said loudly. "Fairies used to practice all types of magic and have the same lifespan, before the council was formed fairies were free to explore any magical abilities or focus on a faction of it," she tried to calm herself before the librarian came to scold her. "I don't understand why they changed it. Sure, the more magics you hone the more weaknesses come along with it but you are also capable of so much more. And I hate the idea of being forced into a box, why should my life be defined by one thing?"

"I was reading some of your council history book, really interesting stuff by the way," Mae said sarcastically, making Dori crack the slightest smile. "It was some king's direction to change the system right?"

"Yeah, apparently the queen went dark and limiting to a singular type of magic limits how much darkness can affect you. So the King instructed his children to start the council and that each fairy would be in one faction, that way all fairies would be safer from the D.I.E."

"The die?" Mae asked, astonished.

"It stands for Dark Intent Effect. Each type of magic has its own set of weaknesses but there are also consequences if a fairy uses their magic for bad, or intertwines with darkness," Dori began to explain casually, like reciting a children's story. "For example, there was a sect of Night fairies that rejected their duty to defend the realm and turned to dark magic to increase their power; dark magic consumed them and trapped them in shadow form," Dori added plainly. "Actually a lot of witch magic creatures come from the dark intent effect. Like Gorgons, witches realized they could use dark magic to turn fairies to stone so they created Gorgons based on the weakness of Meta fairies to perform that task more effectively."

"And vampires are witch magic, but not an intentional creation?"

"Correct. The Seraphina witches sought power and technically they did find it. You have strength, speed, and heightened senses like Night fairies, healing ability like Meta fairies, and you're immortal, not exactly sure the origins of that but it had something to do with the ridge."

"Oh! So, the statue at the base of the ridge, that's that King that started the council, right?" Mae asked beginning to connect the dots.

"Yeah," Dori paused a moment. "That's right, you must live in the east!" Dori realized excitedly. "So you've been to the ridge?"

"Well yeah, I mean it's nothing special. Right before we got here some witches and vampires were killed mysteriously performing some ritual so no one really goes past the statue," Mae said plainly.

"Sounds creepy," Dori said, eyes widening a bit not hiding the disgust on her face. "The ridge in Zalor is incredible," Dori continued. "It's like color is more alive there, the stones emanate magic and it's so cool!"

"What do you mean they emanate magic?" Mae asked.

"Well each type of magic has two power gems," Dori paused to think about how to explain it. "They kind of work as a totem, connected to magic itself, a way of honing it's power. Remember how I told you my dad is within the council? Well his boss carries one of the power gems, one of the sun gems. And the other sun gem is in the ridge on the east of the island, in our realm of course."

"So there are 14 gems then? Because there are 7 magics, right?" Mae asked.

"Yes, one with each elder and one in each stone in the ridge. Two of each were formed in ancient times so both the king and queen could each have a crown with one set of the gems. The crowns were passed down for centuries, but when the council was created the gems were separated," Dori said plainly.

"But why put them in the stones?" Mae looked at her friend confused.

"Oh that wasn't done on purpose! Legend says that the queen I was telling you about earlier, Dahlia, attempted to channel the power of the gems on the ridge. The ridge is a revered location in the fae realm because of its ancient ceremonies. So the queen tried to siphon the magic from the power gems using the potency of magic from Lithos Ridge."

Mae's eyes widened as she listened intently.

"Yeah no one really knows exactly how it happened but the crown was definitely destroyed during some kind of incantation. Now it's a golden circle in the middle of the ridge. And some believe the gems were breaking too because there are bits of color leading to each stone on the ridge, it's like large glitter specks paving the way to each stone," Dori said getting lost in her thoughts. "I wish I could show you, but we aren't allowed to take pictures of the ridge because of it's significance."

"Well, actually, there is a way you can show me," Mae offered. Dori looked at her confused. "I don't know how much you know about vampires and their abilities but we can do this thing the witches refer to as Vide Aspectum. So if you let me into your thoughts I can see what you see," Mae said shrugging her shoulders.

Dori paused taking in the information. She looked at her friend, "How does it work?"

Mae sat up and slid her bean bag a little closer to Dori. She looked Dori deep in the eyes, "Picture the ridge, focusing on the details, as if you are there right now," she said raising her hands on either side of Dori's head, hovering a couple inches from each temple. "Now close your eyes, and trust me," she said leaving the word "trust" lingering in the air between them.

Dori shut her eyes gently as Mae placed her hands on Dori's temples. Dori thought of the last time she visited the ridge. Walking through the entrance of the ridge with the Earth magic stones at the entrance, Dryad and Tempes. Dori looked from the intricate vine etchings of the Dryad stone with a glowing green gem sitting amongst the leaves engraved on its face, toward her personal favorite stone to the right of her. The Tempes stone glistened white like freshly fallen snow, with an illusion of storms clouds at the top that magically blended into whatever sky was seen beyond it. Walking more into the circle were the celestial magics, Sun and Night. Dori could get lost in sparkling midnight of the Night stone. She almost forgot she wasn't there. "Is it working?" Dori asked looking around.

Mae pushed a little further and suddenly she appeared next to Dori in the memory holding her hand. She nodded smiling at her best friend, not able to break through enough to speak.

Dori was amazed, but tried to focus on the memory itself so she didn't mess it up. She paused at the opening before leaving the grass and stepping onto the obsidian circle. Any fairy with a sense of honor always gave a slight bow to enter Lithos Ridge, inhaling the power and preforming the hallowed movements of magic. First, arms down for the power of earth, then up to the sky. Dori muttered the words with her eyes closed, as her arms moved smoothly, dancing through the positions. "Earth. Sky. Life," she said pulling her hands to her chest, her fingers widespread as she paused breathing in the word. She exhaled the final word out with her breath, "spirit," as she pushed her hands outward expelling a few glitter sparkles from her fingers.

She walked through the stones to the center showing Mae the golden circle that laid in the middle of the ridge. Dori turned to the right and walked to the Sun stone reaching out and touching the engravings of flame just as she did in the moment where this memory took place, feeling the warm stone on her fingertips. Mae's eyes didn't leave the ground, she was mesmerized by the glittering specks in each stone's respective color, like flecks of broken glass, leading from the golden circle at the center of the ridge to the gem of power locked in each stone. Sitting closest to Mae's feet, was a deep black leading to the Night stone across from where Dori stood and deep mossy green specks leading to the Dryad stone at the entrance to the circle.

But because Mae was in a memory, her eyes were pulled back to Dori, she watched as Dori walked past the Fauna stone with a polished pink gem sitting in the paw of the Dragon etched at its center. Dori stood staring at the Meta stone, and Mae's jaw dropped as she witnessed magic flowing from the large yellow stone into Dori. Dori's chest rose as she inhaled the sparkling air. Mae saw a brief flicker of glitter come from Dori's back in the shape of wings, it was a stunning display of magic in its natural state, breathing energy into the fairy that stood before her.

Dori wanted to turn toward Mae but her body simply moved the way it had before, her head gave a twitch as she attempted to break through to acknowledge her friend but was forced to step away around the yellow stone toward the cliffs. Mae walked past the bright blue Water stone with etchings of magnificent waves encasing a Kraken at its center. Moving around the yellow stone, Mae saw a gold encased woman, hands outstretched to the ocean beyond the ridge. Dori sat at the feet of the statue looking out over the waves, reliving the moment.

Legend says Dahlia became obsessed with power and attempted to increase her lifespan and power with dark magic. When Kairos stopped her they were both immortalized in stone. What didn't make sense to Dori was that when the fae had divided the realm from the human world, Dahlia's stone figure stayed in the magical realm, and Kairos' went to the human side. Dahlia's statue was encased in gold to prevent her spirit from returning to the realm. Dori thought it was overkill but she didn't know much about spirits returning and all that. She was supposed to be past the history portion of her education, but thanks to her father, she had to endure one more year of it in a special elective that would prepare her for the internship she didn't want. Maybe that class could be an opportunity to find out more about the mystery of Queen Dahlia.

Just as Mae started admiring the golden queen standing before her someone dropped a stack of books and both friends jumped and lost the connection. They were pulled back to sitting on their beanbags in the library. Both blinking aggressively Mae pulled her hands away from Dori's face.

"Wow," Mae said gently. "Thank you for showing me that."

Dori just gave a small smile, saddened that she wasn't still sitting out on the ridge listening to the waves.

CHAPTER 12

Doodling in her agenda book while attempting to listen to her Council History Professor spout on about ancient times and magics, Dori couldn't get her brain to quiet down and actually absorb any of today's lesson.

"When the council was formed it took several hundred years to get the population to commit to the factions," the short, pink-haired professor said in a mundane tone.

Dori looked up at the changing slide to make it appear like she was paying attention. Her heart tugged in her chest reminding her of Mae, and the truth she had just learned. How could she be a vampire? Dori had sensed light in her friend, even still after knowing the truth, she knew Mae was good. Dori had never put much belief in the strict rules against entire races of supernatural, there is no way every last supernatural creature that wasn't a fairy could be inherently bad. And hadn't Mae proved that? But it didn't change the fact she was friends with her people's 'enemy'. Someone directly tied to the people who hurt Abigor just days before. Not that he was still hurt. It would be one thing if she was friends with a lost fae, she might get a slap on the wrist and told never to associate with her again, and probably ruin her eligibility for the internship in the tower, tragic. But a vampire!

SMACK! Dori's attention was pulled back to the board as the professor slapped a yard stick against it point to the visuals.

"The Meta stone sits at the center of Lithos ridge as it represents the unity of all magics, as all things have spirit, aura, energy."

"Yet Meta seem to be the weakest of them all," Kenina whispered, not so quietly, to the girl next to her. Dori side eyed her and saw both girls laughing in her direction.

"I admire Meta fairies, willing to open themselves up to greater risk of the darkness, tapping into the spirits, which is why the faction is so small nowadays," the professor continued, not noticing the chatting girls.

"Told yah," Kenina snickered.

Dori fully turned and stared at Kenina but it just made the girl laugh more.

"Is there a problem, ladies?"

Dori turned back to face the front of the classroom but didn't know what took over her as her mouth opened. "Isn't it true Meta used to be the leaders of the realm before the council?"

"Yes, the royal families were often strongest in Meta as access to the spirits created the ability to blend magics," the professor answered plainly.

Dori again felt like she wasn't in control of herself and turned to smile at Kenina raising her eyebrows in triumph.

"But, sadly, we all know what happened to the last royal family," the professor uttered with a sigh. "Intertwining magics has many benefits, but also opens us up to more weaknesses. But that is exactly why we must know of the D.I.E. and be on the look out for it's warning signs."

"You mean like a sad little Meta fairy pretending to be a Sun fairy," Kenina taunted flicking a sparkle of light from her finger in Dori's direction.

"Now now, let's get back to the task at hand," the professor went on talking about Lithos Ridge and the significance of the stones. Dori's mind was still stuck on the mention of blending magics. She intertwined her magics often, like the invisibility bubble she had just done around Mae a few days ago, the illusion powers of Sun magic, and the dimensional magic from Meta.

"Excuse me professor," Dori said, softly raising her hand. The professor turned from the board and glanced down her nose at Dori, her eyes just gazing over the glasses on the tip of her pointed nose. "You mentioned blending magics, could you expand more on that?" Kenina scoffed on the other side of the room.

The professor gave a shrug, "I suppose it does relate to today's lesson in lost magics," she said waving her hand over the board bringing back the timeline slide that was up before. "Many fairies had the ability to intertwine their magics. As we all understand, secondary magics are utilized to enhance the primary magic. For example, I am a Fauna fairy, but my secondary magic is Dryad, so not only do I communicate with living beings but I also communicate with the living world. So I am able to listen to the earth and help nurture animals better because of that. Often times a Meta fairy might want to have Fauna as a secondary to enhance their healing and empathic abilities."

Dori listened intensely and half of the class was more attentive as well.

"Some fairies were so talented in intertwining magics, it was very difficult to convince them of the new regime when the council was introduced, because it meant surrendering much of their power."

"Like the lost powers?" A Water fairy in the back asked.

"Yes, the ability to intertwine magics resulted in many of the now 'lost' powers. Stemming from energy magic, these fairies could channel any energy, whereas now we channel with one another to achieve those stronger abilities. Why we need many Sun to come together for Solar Augmentation, or many Meta coming together to utilize the dimensional magic. Multiple fairies provide the energy needed to perform enhanced magic that is now lost."

The dimensions. Dori's mind went back to her closet, and explaining to Mae her ability to create this dimension all on her own.

"Wait, so no fairies can do those magics on their own anymore?" Another student asked. Dori leaned in, listening intently as she was wondering the same thing.

"No, that's why they are lost," the professor said, with a derisive tone. "Without energy magic the abilities are too great for one fairy to achieve. Now we spend years honing our craft, which allows us to become more powerful. I have known one Night fairy to hone his power enough to nearly accomplish a supernova before he died," she continued, pausing a moment as if remembering the fairy. "But that's extremely rare, and he spent his entire 700 years only devoted to Celestial Magic, and some believe channeling the power to attempt the Supernova is what led to his death."

"But wouldn't that technically mean we are less powerful now?" the girl with apricot hair sitting next to Kenina asked. Kenina let out a scoff as if completely over the discussion.

"No, let's remember the faction system was put in place to protect us, With less weakness, we are, in fact, stronger," the professor answered, pausing to let her words sink in. "Which brings us back to the Magic Revolution!" she exclaimed, happy to be back on topic.

Dori could barely hear her professor continue talking about the end of the royal family and surrendering power as her mind raced with possibilities. She had always challenged her magic, studied hard and tried to push the limits of her abilities. But had always thought it was Meta and Sun she was tapping into, definitely not one of the lost magics. But she was in fact able to perform magic that took many fairies channeling one another to accomplish. She thought back to putting her backpack in her locker that morning; she hadn't had time to empty the contents and the sparkling black pants shimmered in the lights of the hallway, mocking her and she aggressively pushed her bag in grabbing her books for class. They hadn't turned back to denim, and now that she thought about it, many of the fabrics she worked with she had altered entirely, not just color but the very fabric itself. Could she be utilizing substance magic all on her own?

Maybe she was just naturally good at Meta magic, and able to hone into the specifics of Meta earlier than most. Her mind went to the mention of Sun Augmentation. Light was easy for any fairy with Sun magic to manipulate, but control over intensity of sunlight required many Sun fairies. But that was the same for dimensional magic requiring many Meta. Dori gazed out the window, now with a burning desire to see what she could do with sunlight.

Mae. She thought. *My best friend can't go into sunlight. But if I can control sunlight—*

Dori completely lost focus as a wild idea came to mind. Things were still weird between her and Mae but maybe this was a way to show how much she meant to her, that their kin didn't make a difference to their friendship. Dori began aggressively scribbling in her notebook.

Mae paced back and forth in the coffee shop loft. Conrad kept shouting up at her to calm down. She was already on her second iced mocha, there was no calming down. Dori hadn't said much of what she was planning, she had had a very busy week with school and whatever surprise she was working on, so she hadn't had any time to see Mae. They had been texting throughout the week some, but things still felt off and Mae couldn't wait to finally hang out again to clear the air. Now that their secrets were on the table they had much more to discuss. But Dori wouldn't budge on what she was planning, Mae hated surprises and had been dying to know more all week. Dori just asked Mae to meet her at the coffee shop the morning of the Harvest Festival, with no information on what for.

There were decorations covering every bit of the northern part of the island; Mae wasn't the only one up before the sun, tons of people and fairies were rushing to finish all the preparations. There were pumpkins everywhere, stalks of corn, scarecrows, garlands made of yellow, orange, and red leaves. If there was a fall decoration known to man , it was on this island.

The Bitter Brew Box was no exception, Conrad avoided unwanted attention because of his particular clientele, so he had to put up some decorations or be a sore thumb in a sea of autumn. The Harvest Festival created a slow day whereas usually this time of year was very busy for him, being that his café is gothic themed year round. Adding some black pumpkins, bats and a little haunted house on the counter was all he needed to make it perfect for spooky season. He even added some black and purple bulb string lights to the ceiling this year, honestly they were a nice touch he could leave up all year if he wanted, Mae was admiring them when she heard the door open. She sped down the spiral staircase and in a blur was facing her friend coming through the entryway.

Dori's head jerked back. "Woah. Sorry that's the first time I've seen you do that," she said, amazed.

"It's just Conrad here and he knows about supernatural so no need to hide," Mae said pointing to the empty café behind her. "Now what's going on," she uttered sternly looking Dori directly in the eyes.

Dori smiled. "Hold on a minute," she said to Mae before walking past her. "Conrad, do you have any harvest specials?"

Mae turned throwing her head back and gave a begrudging "uhhhhhhh".

"For you, gorgeous, anything," Conrad said putting his book down and starting up the espresso machine.

Dori turned toward Mae and perked up on her toes as she pulled something from her pocket and put it behind her back. "So I have a weird question," she said to her friend.

Mae scowled at Dori. "As long as it has something to do with your plan."

"So, you can't do sun, but like do you burst into flame the instant sun hits your skin or is it more of a slow burn?" Dori asked.

Mae looked appalled. "What kind of—"

"Just answer the question," Dori interrupted.

Mae glared and let out a sigh. "It's more like your skin boils and then you burst into flame. It's not instant but it's still relatively quick," she said bluntly.

"Okay good," Dori smiled. "Put this on." She pulled her hands from behind her back and tossed something to Mae.

Mae nimbly caught the necklace that her friend tossed in her direction. She held out her hand and let the necklace dangle from her fingers. A blue stone that flickered with green shimmer in the light hung in a perfect circle in the clutch of a silver dragon claw. Mae went to speak but Dori's stare stopped her and she did as she was directed.

"Great! Now time to test it!" Dori said excitedly as she began pushing Mae toward the door.

"TEST IT?" Mae exclaimed. She was fighting Dori but even though she was the stronger one of the two of them Dori must have been using her magic because she was gliding quickly toward the door. She stumbled through the first door into the vestibule. Dori jumped around and put her hand on the front door leading outside.

"If this doesn't work I am sorry," Dori said as she opened up the door leading outside.

Mae threw her hands up to cover her face as the sun rays came bursting through the open door. But no heat came. She slowly pulled her hands down, gazing at the sunlight on her skin in amazement. The hint of olive in her skin glistened in the sunlight as she rolled her hands in the air observing every fleck of light that hit her skin. "How did you—" she began to question but was stopped in pure awe of what was happening.

"The other day we were talking about mixing magic in class, and I figured if I could create a sort of dimensional protection from the sun rays then theoretically it could protect you from harm. And well, it worked," Dori said with a slight squeal.

Mae looked at her friend tenderly. "Thank you," she said. Dori smiled. "No really, Dori you have no idea what this means to me," Mae said touching her friends arm and the necklace.

"Now, it's really important that no one knows about this. This kind of magic, and a fairy helping a vampire will bring a lot of unwanted attention and I could get in a lot of trouble."

"Promise," Mae said without hesitation.

"Okay," Dori smiled at her friend. "Soooo, wanna go to the Harvest Festival?" Dori asked with a giddy little jump.

Mae's face lit up with excitement, and Conrad appeared behind the duo coffee in hand. Mae looked at him, with threat looming in her eyes. "Don't worry, you're secrets safe with me," he said calming both their nerves.

"Good. Because you know I'd rip your throat out," Mae said proudly taking one of the coffees from Conrad's hands, as she flashed her pearly white fangs.

Conrad handed Dori her coffee, ignoring Mae. "Sick charm, well done," he complimented.

"Thanks," Dori said proudly, grabbing the coffee. "Ready?" She asked turning her attention to Mae.

Turning her gaze to the open door, sunlight pouring in. All her nerves were screaming not to take that step forward. Mae stepped to the door, took a deep breath and stepped out onto the sidewalk.

It was about 9 o'clock, the sun was high in the sky; Mae looked around taking everything in like it was the very first time she had been outside. It had been 200 years since she had the sun on her skin, she felt human again, the sun was warm on her skin but nothing more. She stared at her arm waiting for it to start burning, she must be dreaming because here she was, outside with the day breeze moving past her. The smell of caramel apples and pumpkins filled her lungs. The Harvest Festival had just opened, though most people wouldn't be arriving for another couple hours. The only people around were those attending the festival booths and involved in performances. Mae and Dori would be some of the first few to the festival, which calmed Mae a bit knowing she wouldn't be in a big crowd.

Dori linked her arm around Mae's and led her through the festival. They took their time hitting the different booths and enjoying every little bit of the festivities. They got to a booth with a familiar face.

"Hey Opal!" Dori said, hugging the short stocky woman organizing trinkets on the fold out tables.

"Endora! Oh let me look at you," Opal said pushing Dori back into view holding tight to each arm. "Are you really a senior this year?"

"Yup! I'm actually a TA for Lenora," Dori responded with glee.

"I always knew you'd be the top of your class," Opal smiled at Dori then turned her attention to Mae, her dark auburn curls bouncing around her face. "Who's your friend?"

"Oh, sorry! Opal this is Mae," Dori said stepping back next to her friend. "Mae this is Opal. She's kind of like an older sister. We grew up next door to each other, until she moved all the way across the city," Dori added teasing Opal, "And our moms are best friends."

"Hi," Opal said before her gaze fell upon the pendant hanging from Mae's neck. "Interesting necklace you have there," she said reaching out for it. Mae got a little shiver as Opal's fingers touched the necklace.

"Thanks, it was a gift from Dori," Mae said a little skittish.

Opal side eyed Dori, "How nice of her," she looked back at Mae and gave a coy smile. Then she leaned into Dori giving her another hug, "I added a magic blocker to your charm, that way fairies can't sense the magic. Be careful who you share that magic with, I hope your friend is trustworthy," she whispered in her ear, giving Mae a gentle side eye glance.

Dori pulled back from the hug and mouthed 'thank you' to Opal.

"Don't worry, I won't tell a soul," Opal said. "Now go enjoy the festival," she said to both girls.

"It was nice meeting you," Mae said to Opal, who simply gave an approving nod.

The girls walked silently toward the giant pumpkin display in the middle of the town square. Mae simply looked at Dori waiting for an explanation.

"Right, I forgot you have super hearing so you heard that," Dori said shaking her head, she was still getting used to the fact her best friend was a vampire. "Opal is also a Meta fairy," Dori said under her breath. "She could probably sense the magic emanating off the stone, and since you have an aura of darkness she deduced what you are. Her blocker will prevent anyone else from doing that."

"So we are good?" Mae asked, a tad confused.

"Yeah, actually really good. The new combination of charms will make you appear like either a young fairy, with low aura of magic, or as a human. Any fairies you pass by won't be able to tell you are a magical being," Dori said. "So you are free to roam about during the day without any lingering fairies getting in your business."

The word free hung in the air around Mae for a minute. Her mind raced with all the possibilities, then one came up fast bringing her mind to a halt.

She could leave.

CHAPTER 13

Mae stood there frozen. Dori kept walking toward the pumpkin display and did a double take when she realized her friend was no longer next to her.

"What is it?" Dori said, walking back toward Mae.

Mae's eyes weren't focusing and she looked past Dori into space. Awakening at the touch of Dori's hand on her arm, she looked down at the hand holding her then up at her friend. "I'm free," Mae looked deep into Dori's eyes as a tear welled up in her eye. "Dori, I can leave the island."

"Would you?" Dori responded without thinking. She never thought much about how trapped her friend must feel. She spent enough time near the village on the east to know it couldn't be very spacious, and her friend was 200 years older than her, trapped in a house with a family who constantly belittled her. They had that in common, it had been one of the many things that forged their bond, but Dori couldn't imagine enduring all she did at home for centuries. Of course Mae would want to leave the island. Go somewhere where she could live a normal life. Dori hadn't thought that far ahead when creating the necklace, just that she would be able to walk in the sun, that her friend would be able to go to the Harvest Festival with her. How could she be so short-sighted.

Mae looked at her friend and could tell she had caused her mind to race as well. "I would love to, but this is all so new, I don't know what to do with the possibilities," she paused a moment and decided this all could be dealt with later. "Let's just focus on today," she said smiling at Dori.

Dori smiled back at her, knowing how much Mae probably wanted to just run right now and never look back, but was thankful that they could enjoy the day.

They wandered around the festival, taking pictures together, gandering through the items in the booths, and eating corndogs and apple cider donuts. Although Mae quickly realized they were coated with cinnamon sugar and spat hers out while choking.

Dori held back a laugh as she took another bite of her donut. "So I guess we should stay clear of the churro cart," she said smiling at Mae.

Mae glared and stuck her tongue out. The girls continued walking arm in arm laughing and enjoying the day. The crowds got a bit bigger and they were about to leave when someone shouted "Dori!"

Dori's eyes got wide knowing who the voice belonged to. "Who is it?" Mae asked her.

But it was too late to escape now, Jareth was standing right behind them. "Hey, woah who's your friend?" His attention automatically turning to Mae, looking her up and down with all the subtlety of a dragon scorching through the arctic.

"Mae, meet Jareth," Dori said less than pleased.

"Mae, a pleasure. I'm Dori's big brother," he said ironically as he stood a couple inches shorter than his sister. He grabbed Dori and side hugged her despite her resistance. "What have you and my little sister been up to? Enjoying the festival?"

"Actually we were just leaving," Dori replied.

"But I just got here, come on let me hang out with you and your friend," he said looking Mae up and down again.

Mae gave a small smirk. "We've got somewhere else to be," she said grabbing Dori's hand and pulling her from beside her brother. She looked at her watch, "Ooh and we are late too. Bye." She said not hiding her disgust at the boy who stood before them. She turned and pulled Dori behind her through the crowd back toward the café.

Waiting until they were through the crowd to let out her breath, Mae turned to Dori eyes wide.

"Dude, seriously. Instant rage. The urge to kill, so intense," Mae exclaimed dramatically.

"I know. I'm sorry. He seriously has no tact," Dori said.

"I mean, it wasn't even flattering! Does he not hear himself?" Mae shuddered repulsed by the interaction.

"This is why I tend not to bring my friends home, only if I know he's not there. Nice save getting us out of there by the way," Dori said.

"Yeah, I knew I couldn't hang around him any longer, I could actually rip his stupid little head off," Mae said twisting her fists together and making a ripping motion.

Dori laughed and they walked back into the café. They told Conrad all about their adventures at the festival

"Wow, your brother sounds like a real treat," Conrad said dramatically. "When do I get to meet him?" he mocked as he poured them a new drink he had been working on.

Dori and Mae laughed at him rolling their eyes. "I didn't even want poor Mae here to be cursed with his presence," Dori said apologetically.

"So I call this the Blue Dragon, it's got dragon fruit, blue raspberry and a choice of lemonade or sparkling lemon water if you want it fizzy," Conrad said smiling, handing each girl a version of the drink.

"Oh my, this is my new favorite thing," Mae said, drinking nearly half in one breath.

"Ooooohhh I like the fizzy version! Delicious! Great job Conrad," Dori said smiling.

"Thanks, I love having a day where I can work on new concoctions, next I'll be working on some Winter

Solstice drinks just for you, Dori," Conrad said, giving her a playful wink.

Dori jumped up excited, Mae rolled her eyes at her friend and they both walked to a table. Dori looked over at Mae, "Hey I just noticed, how come your eyes aren't black?"

Mae looked across the table at her friend, eyebrows raised, "Why would my eyes be black?"

"Because you're a vampire, I thought all vampires eyes were black," Dori said.

Mae thought about that for a moment, "I mean my dad's are black, but the rest of my family has normal eye colors."

"It's because he chose to become a vampire," Conrad said, from across the café not even looking up from the glasses he was cleaning.

"What?" Both girls asked simultaneously.

Conrad looked up at them, "Yeah, only vampires who choose to become vampires have black eyes, anyone who was forced to turn keeps their human eyes," he explained.

"How do you know that?" Mae asked.

"I've been on Delmira island a long time Mae, and run a café with tempered glass windows, you learn a thing or two about the supernatural," Conrad said with a chuckle.

Dori looked at Mae and shrugged. "Your dad is the only one who chose to be a vampire right?"

"Yeah, I guess that makes sense. And the girl that just moved here has blue eyes, and she was turned by her boyfriend. How have I been around so long and never knew this?" Mae questioned.

"It's why Zagan will never trust you, why your dad is allowed in his mansion and you're not," Conrad said.

Mae and Dori both stared at him in disbelief.

"Like I said, you learn a lot being the vamps' favorite café. Plus witches like to gossip," he said, returning to his dishes.

Mae looked over at Dori, "I underestimated him," she said and they both laughed.

Dori's face fell ever so slightly, "So do you think you'd want to leave now that you're not stuck here?"

Mae took a long pause staring at her friend, "This is still all so fresh, I don't really know what I want to do."

Dori dropped her eyes, thinking about how much she cared for her friend and what her leaving would look like. "I guess that makes sense, lots to consider."

Mae reached across the table touching her friend's arms, "No matter what happens, nothing will change between us Dori," she said smiling, "You're stuck with me."

Dori looked up at Mae, hoping with everything she had that this friendship would last, but her insecurities screamed at her, people never stayed, no one would love her forever, everyone eventually left.

And she had just handed a reason to leave right to the most important person in her life.

CHAPTER 14

Walking in the door, eyes beaming, despite the lingering wonder of the future Dori had an amazing day with Mae. They explored more of the island and enjoyed all the time the sun gave them. To keep up appearances, Mae joined her fellow vampires after sunset wandering around the island. Dori had been working hard all week and after a day on her feet, couldn't wait for a long hot shower and to snuggle up in her bed.

But of course it couldn't be that simple, instead she arrived home to Jareth, waiting for her, and no one else around to create a buffer.

"How was the thing you had to run off to?" Jareth asked skeptical.

"It was great, thanks," Dori replied, attempting to cut the conversation there, but she knew better than to think it could be that simple.

"Tell me more about your friend, do you think we would get along?"

She had only stepped on the first stair when she stopped short; he couldn't possibly be going where she thought it was going. She didn't want to encourage him by telling him anything about Mae, she would have preferred to say something about him not getting along with anyone but held her tongue. "Why do you ask?" She asked turning back around to face him.

"Are you kidding? She's hot! You should set us up on a date," Jareth said as if instructing her.

"I thought you didn't date humans?" Dori said with a smirk, knowing they would be having a completely different conversation if Jareth knew what Mae actually was.

"When someone looks as amazing as your friend, you make an exception. I'm not asking to marry her, but we could have some fun," he said with a chuckle.

Dori was dumbfounded, even after living with him her entire life he still amazed her with how idiotic he could be. "So let me get this straight, you want me to set you up with my friend, who you have no intention of having a real relationship with, so *you* can have some 'fun,'" she said using air quotes. "Because you think she's hot."

"What's the big deal? I'm a fun guy to hang around with, we can go to some of the upcoming holiday parties and have a good time," Jareth said.

"I'm not going to set you up," Dori said shaking her head and turning back to walk up the stairs.

"Why do you always shut me out from everyone in your life? You and Blythe are so determined to cut me out of everything!" He said beginning to raise his voice. "What did I ever do to you?"

Don't do it. Don't freak out. Just let it go.

Dori's mind told her. But her anger roared within her. She turned around looking at him from halfway up the stairs. "Are you serious? You constantly insult us, yell at us, hurt everyone around you, why would we want to share anything with you?" Dori said waiting for a genuine answer to her questions.

"You always leave me out, you act like you are so much better than me, meanwhile you're the one palling around with a worthless human at a fairy festival. I don't understand what you want from me." Jareth said, angrily.

"How about not calling my friend worthless for one?" Dori said amused.

"She's a human. They are the lesser species. You spend your time hanging out with humans, wanting a life out there in their world and you still somehow think you are superior to me?"

"I don't judge someone by what species they are, *or* the type of magic they choose," Dori said with a hiss. Jareth always judged their mother for being a Meta fairy and hated Dori's love for that magic. He viewed Meta fairies as servants; all they did was care for other people, never doing anything for themselves. He believed caring for others, especially humans, was a weakness and that Meta fairies were the weakest fairies caring for the human world so dearly. "So maybe I do think I'm better than you because I'm not an *asshole*," she spat out the word letting it hang in the air.

"Wow what a big word! Are you allowed to say things like that, doesn't it ruin your goody-goody lifestyle?" Jareth's voice went from mockery to crisp as he took steps up toward his sister. "You are nothing! You will never *be* anything," he practically spat in her face, hissing the words inches from her face. "You don't even know what you want to do with your life or what magic you want to do! Because you are a stupid child that thinks she's some hot power," he screamed now staring her right in the face, his piercing blue eyes like a dagger in her spirit along with his words. "Dad thinks you'll be some great thing for the future of the council but we both know you'll just do whatever Abigor wants of you. You'll be a good little wife and Abigor will run everything," Jareth said laughing, "I bet you don't even get the internship."

Dori did everything in her power not to cry right on the spot. "You're wrong," she muttered.

Jareth just laughed at her calmly. "And you are a joke. Whatever, Dori. You're not worth a second of my time," he said, backing down the stairs. "You enjoy your human friend, I'll be better off without both of you."

Dori swallowed what felt like a rock in her throat. She stared as he walked down the stairs and into the living room. Turning, she dragged her feet up the remaining stairs to her bedroom. She closed the door and let her body fall against it sinking to the ground. Hugging her knees, her chest tight, she whimpered trying not to make a sound. Picking her head up ever so slightly to eye her closet just a few feet to the left, if she could make it in there she could scream and let her emotions out. But she was paralyzed with dread. She heard the TV turn on downstairs and was thankful knowing she could cry without being heard. Her jaw fell open in a silent cry as she begged for a better life, collapsing further into the floor. Her sobs rang in her head until she could barely breathe and her face was soaked with her tears. She pulled her head from her knees looking up at her room, hating the very sight of everything around her; then the pain began and she slowly fell to the side letting her pain overcome her. She wasn't sure how much time passed before her mind came out of the fog of unending pain.

Yearning for freedom, she tried to imagine a better life after she graduated, but Jareth was right, she didn't know what she would do, let alone where she would go to escape this house. One thing was certain though, she couldn't stay here. Then she thought of Mae, who yearned to leave this island possibly more than she did. Maybe the two of them could go off to college some-where, live normal lives away from their families.

Dori lost herself in the day dream of a better life, just her and her best friend. She sat silent against the door not even realizing the hours ticking by. She finally crawled up onto her bed and pulled the blankets up to her face. Her head pounding from crying, feeling empty, lost, and yet somehow like nothing at all. She eventually succumbed to sleep, hoping that dream land would be nicer than her living nightmare.

Watching the other students leave class, Dori sat patiently watching Professor Lenora sort through papers on her desk. She had assumed that Lenora was going to give her more work to do, since she had finished all her TA assignments already, but was confused as to why she had been asked to wait until all other students were out of the classroom.

The large wooden doors closed shut with the last student and Lenora picked her head up from her work as if on cue. Dori was still sitting front row in the stadium style desks and watched her professor look past her, double checking no others still remained. Lenora waved her hand in the direction of the front door creating a barrier of glittery yellow. Dori looked from the professor to the door and back. Now she was concerned. Whatever Lenora wanted to talk to her about must be pretty important to take that extra step of keeping people out.

Lenora stared at Dori, "It's not just a barrier," she said. "It provides us privacy so no one can overhear our discussion." Dori kept the blank stare on her face, afraid to speak until asked. Lenora walked from behind her desk toward Dori in the front row. "I hear you have quite the talent in dimensional magic, and you've decided to share that with a vampire."

How?

Dori's mouth fell open just barely but no words came out. She racked her brain to try and figure out how Lenora knew about the necklace. Besides her and Mae, only Conrad and Opal knew about it.

Lenora could see the concern on Dori's face, "Don't fret, Endora. I have no intention of sharing this information with anyone." Dori let out a sigh of relief. "In fact I recommend you make absolutely sure that no one else finds out," Lenora said, taking a seat next to Dori. "Do you understand the type of magic you are using?"

Dori looked at her confused, "I combined my Sun and Meta abilities," she said nervously.

Lenora sat back in her seat examining her student, "Endora," she said slowly. "Do you know why you have purple in your hair?"

Dori grabbed at the tips of her hair looking down at it, staying silent assuming Lenora wasn't actually looking for an answer. Dori thought back to when the purple first appeared in her hair, it had just emerged on the tips of her hair one morning a couple years ago, around the time she created the charm on her closet. Her mom freaked out, going on about ruining her beautiful blonde hair and not having permission to magically alter her body. Adelyn was very against body adaptations other than ones that came naturally from magic, Dori didn't understand why magic could choose to adapt your appearance but it was an atrocity if someone used magic to add a marking or color to their body. She was so upset Dori didn't even get to explain she hadn't dyed it.

"The purple in your hair, and the flecks present in your wings signify the weaving of magic, also known as alchemy magic," Lenora spoke slowly as if allowing

Dori to absorb all she was telling her. "Alchemy magic used to be common, when fairies were allowed to possess multiple magics. In the centuries since dividing into factions that type of magic was lost. You've learned about the lost magics in other classes correct?"

Dori simply nodded.

"The ability to infuse magics together is very powerful, and do you know what powerful fairies open themselves up to?"

"Darkness."

"Darkness indeed," Lenora stood again facing the towering windows overlooking the courtyard, layered with leaves of every color and fairies flying back and forth rushing to their next class. She stood hands folded behind her back, Lenora titled her head to the side to bring Dori into view. "This friend of yours, you trust her?"

Dori stood and began to approach her professor. "Yes. Completely," Dori said without hesitation.

"Endora," Lenora said, turning around grabbing ahold of Dori's arms. "This power you possess is incredible, figuring out how to make that talisman was extremely intuitive of you, and I am very proud."

Dori began to smile but her face fell when Lenora continued.

"But I must warn you to be *very* cautious. No one must know you possess this power, and I urge you to be vigilant of *who* you use it for. I hope you are right about your friend, and you make sure she knows that no other vampires know of this discovery," Lenora urged, staring deep into Dori's eyes. "Powerful magic can be traced, and I'm not the only one with my eye on you."

Dori swallowed hard. "I will make sure," she said firmly. "But why can no one know about the alchemy power, we just learned about intertwining magics in class, isn't it a good thing to have rediscovered lost power?"

Lenora squeezed Dori's arms tighter in her grip. "No," she said insistently. "Darkness is all around us, and it will seek out the most powerful being in attempts to use that power. Endora," she said, her voice lowering to a hush, "there are fairies out there that will seek to use you for dark things, and if you do not oblige—" she paused contemplating her next words carefully. "They will attempt to take that power from you."

"Is that even possible? I know one fairy can channel another but how would—"

"It is very possible, and some fairies have been trying to find someone like you for the very purpose of taking control of your power. There is so much you do not know and I need you to promise me you will not use this type of magic lightly."

"What do you mean fairies are looking for someone like me? What fairies? What do they want the power for?" Dori asked, frantic at the thought.

"That's not important right now. Listen to me, you share this magic with no one. I will help you learn more and control this magic so you will be safe. You have so much potential and can do great things, but no one can know," Lenora said, finally releasing Dori's arms. "Now. Go, you've got other classes to get to, we will talk more another time."

Dori did as she was told while her mind ran wild with all that Lenora had said.

Walking down the stone corridor not able to hide the distress from her face; it was moments like these when she didn't mind being invisible. Her fellow students passed her by without a second thought, some buzzing past her nearly getting caught in her hair as they flew past. Autopilot took over and Dori kept moving down the amber cathedral stairs toward her next class. Class-mates were just blurs of different colors passing her by.

Could she really be in some kind of danger? When she made the necklace the worst she thought was the council would write her off as a sympathizer and she would have to do something like community service as penance. She never imagined she would become a target. She was just one little fairy, caught between two magics, which made her weak, that's what she'd been told all her life. Pick a main magic and you could use a secondary to enhance it. Sure the pendant was a pretty equal share between the two magics but how was that really any different? Why would the discovery of it be a danger to her? What could it be used for that Lenora would be so adamant about her keeping it a secret. She made a pendant, yes a challenging feat but did it really mean she was that powerful? None of this made any sense, and Dori was afraid to ask any of the million questions rolling around in her head.

CHAPTER 15

It was weeks before Lenora set up another time for her and Dori to meet. Lenora had a beach house in the north, outside of Meltembra, that they would meet at. Considering Professor Lenora was 530 years old, Dori expected an old home, still put together of course because Annonette was far too sophisticated to have broken shutters or a rickety porch. Dori was amazed to arrive at one of the newer modern homes on the island. Must've only been built a few years prior. There was a large grey paved driveway leading to the towering glass entryway. Beautiful walls of stained oak and maple, the entire north wall made up of windows overlooking the ocean, lofted over the hill the home safely sat in. Modern art was on almost every wall and surface, even the furniture was very new age, and rather ordinary, Dori thought to herself. Not much signs of fairies here, besides the gorgeous natural plants in every corner, blooming extra vibrantly despite the lack of sunshine this time of year. No personal effects either, except one little picture on the wall, of what appeared to be a young Annonette on her wedding day, next to a strapping young man. Dori was about to ask about the picture, not knowing Lenora was ever married, but Lenora's energy was stale and Dori was afraid to pry.

Dori was ecstatic when Lenora finally asked Dori to perform some magic after they had spent the previous two meetings just talking.

"Okay, now you mentioned being able to conjure your closet at home no matter where you are, correct?"

"Yes," Dori responded with glee. "It's like transforming a wall into the opening of my closet and I can access anything inside,"

"Let's see it," Lenora said gracefully pointing to the tall oak wall next to her.

Dori did as directed and with a purple sparkling burst her closet appeared in the wall beside. Dori reached in and pulled out a blouse to show Lenora. "I can grab anything from it."

Lenora observed the yellow framed closet in her oak wall. After a long minute of silence. "Now picture something you've lost, a piece of jewelry, shirt, whatever it may be."

"Umm, oh! I did have this purple shirt with gold accents on the front, it had a criss-cross back to it and was soooo comfortable! I have no idea where that went!"

Lenora smiled at her pupil. "Picture it, bring it to the front of your mind," Lenora paused watching Dori concentrate. "Now grab it from your closet."

"But it's not in there, trust me I've looked every-where for that thing!"

Lenora simply gestured to the glowing closet.

Dori shrugged, closing her eyes to pull her focus back. Eyes still shut she reached her hand into the wall, wiggling her fingers, they grasped cloth and she pulled her hand out. Opening her eyes her jaw dropped at the sight of her lost shirt.

"But—" Dori stammered.

"Endora, where do we get the name *Meta* fairy from?"

"It is derived from the aspects of metaphysics," Dori replied, barely looking up from the shirt.

"Which entails?"

"Ummm," Dori thought, looking up counting the characteristics off using her fingers. "It covers the concepts of knowing, space, substance," she paused squeezing her face as she tried to picture the remaining words in the definition she was taught years ago. "Cause and identity!"

"And time," Lenora gracefully added.

"Right, I always forget that one because it's not really a power Meta fairies possess," Dori said with a shrug.

Lenora smiled. "Sweet Endora," she spoke slowly, stepping closer to the young fairy. "It is a power *you* possess. How do you think you were able to reclaim an item you have not seen for some time?"

Dori looked at her amazed.

"Meta fairies have lost the ability to utilize all aspects of their power, they focus on spirit, emotion, healing, and have lost the cornerstones which give us those powers," Lenora said with air of inspiration and an aftertaste of disappointment. "Identity is a pinnacle aspect of our Meta magic, and greatly affects our connection to the Einwhai; without it we cannot reach our full potential. The sheer fact you can utilize dimensional magic shows just how powerful you are, my dear."

"So this is just Meta magic? Not Alchemy?"

"We will get there, I believe you have this ability, and the ability to mix your magics, because it comes from your heart, it is something you feel deeply. Your connection to clothes because of your designing, your desire to help your friend in creating that pendant. You have begun tapping into things you do not understand because you *wanted* it. If you can continue to pursue your true self, you can accomplish anything."

The words sat heavy on her shoulders, she contemplated the truth in Lenora's words as she made the journey back into Zalor.

Dori walked into her house and greeted her mother who was sitting in the living room reading.

"Hey sweetie, where've you been?"

"Working on some class stuff with Professor Lenora," Dori smiled putting her backpack down by the couch and took a seat. "Where is everybody?"

"Dad and Blythe took the dog out for hike, and I'm not sure where Jareth went off to."

Dori nodded acknowledging the answer and awkwardly rubbed her hands together in her lap. "What are you reading?" She asked trying not to leave the silence open too long.

"It's a book called *Mindful Peace* my friend recommended for me," Adelyn said excitedly. "It's interesting, all about looking inward and cultivating peace," she added picking up the book and flipping through a few pages.

Dori should be proud of her for trying to work on herself, but knew she probably wouldn't read too much of the book, or apply any of it to her life. Her mother lived in a blissful state, ignoring the problems around her. Maybe it was better that way. "Sounds like a great read," she offered.

"When is Abigor's party tonight? Did you make anything special for the occasion?"

"Not til 6, but I've gotta start getting ready soon and go early to help set up. I haven't really had time to sew recently so I didn't make anything though," Dori said, a little saddened, she had been so distracted by everything lately she hadn't had any time for designing and thinking about it made her miss it even more.

"Do you want help getting ready? I know I don't have the fashion taste you do but maybe let your old mom have a crack at it?"

Dori gave a half-smile, she appreciated those moments her mom tried, and always jumped at the opportunity. She longed for a normal mother-daughter relationship, and held to the moments where she could pretend they could have that. Dori watched her mom's reddish curls bounce off her shoulders as they ascended the stairs. Entering Dori's little room, Adelyn sat on Dori's bed looking through the jewelry box she had given her a few years prior. Dori began shifting through her closet and tried on a few different outfits to see what she wanted to wear.

"How have things been going with you and Abigor?"

"Pretty good actually," Dori replied, still sorting through her closet. "We had hit some rough spots but I think things have turned out," she added, trying not to get too into it. It was true there were some rough spots but Dori felt like she was finding herself lately, and truly felt like her relationship was benefiting from that.

"That's good. Relationships take work and you have to be able to work through rough spots," Adelyn exhaled. "You and Abigor really are a beautiful couple and he's become a part of this family, you found a good one there, honey."

Dori lowered her head, hiding her face in the clothes hanging before her, Mae's voice echoed in her head. Her mom had watched her and Abigor together over the years, so she ought to have a better idea of her relationship than Mae would, and Dori often envied the dedication her parents had to one another. Though her mom had a tendency to forget the bad; plus she thought Dori and Jareth were friends, so her perspective couldn't really be trusted. Dori shook her head attempting to focus on the task at hand. "How about this?" Dori asked her mom, as she pulled at the dark blue flowy top she was wearing. She paired it with dark jeans with some sparkle accents down the sides.

"Adorable! Did you make that?"

"Yeah, like a year ago I think," Dori answered admiring the fabric in her hands.

"You really do have a talent for design, Endora," Adelyn said, admiring her.

"Thanks, mom," Dori said, a little giddy.

"Your dad and I are really proud of you."

Dori looked down holding her words back. She wanted to believe that, but she knew her dad would never approve of her doing anything with this particular talent.

"Your dad and your brother were just talking about you doing the internship and what an amazing opportunity it is," Adelyn continued.

Dori turned back to her closet so she could roll her eyes without her mother noticing. Dori knew exactly what she was referencing, Blythe was home when the 'conversation' was had. Jareth had been on an aggressive rant about how his little sister was getting an opportunity she didn't deserve and he should work with the council. Jareth had always been jealous of her successes and never thought she deserved any of it. The fact he failed out of high school the year prior kept eating at him now that Dori was on her way to finishing school before him and nearly at the top of her class. Adelyn must've felt the air shift.

"You know your brother loves you," Adelyn said sincerely.

Dori tried not to react so she didn't upset her mother. Jareth hated her, there was no denying that. Except Adelyn, she would never come to terms with the hatred that dwelt within Jareth, especially not for her other children. Even Jareth denied it, always saying how much he loved his little sister, but the moment she did something he didn't like she was his arch nemesis and he would try to tear her down any way possible. Dori tried to shift the conversation completely, "Should I wear comfy shoes or cute boots?" She asked holding up a pair of sneakers and sparkly black boots.

"Always the cute boots, girlfriend," Adelyn said with glee.

Dori rolled with the shift and picked out some accessories and went to finish getting ready in the bathroom to avoid furthering that conversation.

Readying the final touches on decorations, Dori greeted guests as they started to arrive. Abigor had been very busy in the last weeks so they hadn't seen too much of each other, but every time they were together was better than it had been in years. Dori had been coming out of her shell more and felt like Abigor was accepting that. She poured a lot into his party in hopes of kindling this new stage in their relationship and couldn't wait to see the look on his face when he arrived at the party.

The party went off with a bang, as mini fireworks welcomed Abigor into the hall where his birthday party was being held. He was truly surprised at how extravagant Dori had made everything and thanked her with a light kiss on the cheek after saying hello to the guests. Dori smiled ear to ear at his joy and she watched him laugh the night away with his friends. Fairies spent the whole night dancing all around the hall, on the floors, walls, and ceilings. Abigor pulled her in for a dance, spinning and twirling her before busting out into the center of the room as everyone cheered him on while he did twirling back flips and a spinning headstand.

After the party Abigor led Dori away from cleaning up streamers and balloons, allowing his brothers to finish up. The party was held on the hill below the castle in a Night Warriors Command Post. They walked up to the ancient glowing oak that sat by the entrance to the east bridge of the castle. The night sky was lit with the full moon and a clear view of all the stars with the Auroras dancing around them. The water beneath the bridge shimmered with the magic of the night. Dori sat on one of the golden vine swings hanging from the branches of the large oak.

"Dori," Abigor said sitting on the swing next to her, "Thank you again for this amazing night. It was a great birthday."

"I'm glad you liked it. I just wanted to do something extra special for you," Dori said, reaching out for his hand.

Abigor grabbed her hand in his and looked up at her. His face wasn't happy though, Dori looked at him in wonder.

"What is it?"

"Dori, I have to talk to you about something," Abigor said somberly.

Dori worried that he was about to propose, but his voice told her that couldn't possibly be what was happening.

"Things have been different between us lately," Abigor said, taking a long breath. "You're different, and I think that's great but," he paused.

The moment seemed to last an eternity, Dori's heart was screaming. Then he spoke slow and low, and everything changed.

"I don't think I love you anymore."

His words stung worse than a scorporius gecko on a hot summer day.

Dori was frozen, the words repeating in her ears.

"I mean, I don't want to break up," Abigor interjected breaking Dori from her trance. "I think we should take some time over the holidays to see if things change, and reevaluate in the new year. The city expects a proposal soon," he added with a sigh looking away from her.

So you're only staying with me out of duty. Dori wanted to say but her throat still stung from the pain in her heart.

"But I think if we take some time," Abigor continued, "you've got finals coming up, and I've got the warrior tests, so we will talk next semester after things calm down, and go from there," he said giving a little shrug.

Dori opened her mouth but she didn't know what to say. She wanted to ask why, ask what about her changed so much that he could say such things. For the first time in her entire life she started feeling like she belonged and she could be herself. Even if she still felt lost at times she felt like she was discovering a whole new side of herself; apparently Abigor didn't like this Dori.

"I know it's a lot to think about, for now we'll just keep up appearances in public and we will talk again soon," Abigor said dropping Dori's hands and getting up from the swing. "I'm sorry to drop this on you," he said, kissing her on the head. "I'll see you next weekend for the Solstice festival," he added walking away.

Frozen in place, Dori sat there blank and empty. The swing moved ever so slightly in the wind, her only movement a tiny shiver from the cold. The beautiful night seemed to mock her now as she felt so broken. She wanted to cry but no tears came. She just sat lifeless.

Hadn't she been wanting a way out of this relationship a few months ago? Here it was, presented to her, no one could blame her for walking away now. Her mind went back to the time Abigor had broken up with her. They had been together almost a year and another girl caught his interest. He won Dori back a couple months later, she had forgiven him and forgot all about how crushed she was. Here she was, 3 years later crushed again, but it felt worse this time. She had begun to distance herself, feeling lost at his side, and she fought to get back to a good place with him. What more could he want from her?

Her hands were purple from the cold before she finally stood and began to walk home. Another place she didn't belong. She wondered if there was anywhere in the world or Meltembra that she truly belonged. The snow began to drift down on her as she made her way through the city. Dori looked up breathing in the smell of snow in the air. This was her favorite time of year, but she was empty inside. The thought of it pushed a tear from her eye, and it ran down her cold cheek as she dragged herself through the icy weather.

Down the hill, Dori approached Cafe Fortress just as Sprig was locking up.

"Dori," Sprig said as he turned the key in the door. "What are you doing out so late?"

Dori looked at him still unable to speak.

Sprig looked at her pale hands and her dazed eyes, "Are you alright?"

No matter how much she admired Sprig and trusted him, the question shook her out of her depressive trance. "Yeah, sorry," she said cracking a smile, "Long day." She was used to covering up her pain, she wasn't going to stop now, no matter how broken she felt.

Sprig didn't believe her, but he would never push her to tell him. "Can I walk you home?"

Dori nodded giving a small smile. Sprig removed his jacket and threw it over her shoulders. They walked in silence side by side as they made their way through the concourse, then Sprig began telling Dori about the inventory he was doing for the café and the new recipes he had been playing with throughout the week. Dori was happy for the distraction from her pain and encouraged Sprig to bring some of his unique recipes to the shops on the island for the tourists to enjoy. Before she knew it they were through the suburbs and on her little street in the south of the island. She stared at her blue house and the light on in Jareth's room regretting having to walk inside. Taking off his jacket, Dori turned and thanked Sprig for walking her home.

Sprig looked down at his feet and back up at Dori. "Whatever it is," he muttered. "You'll get through it. You're stronger than anyone I've ever known," Sprig said, pursing his lips together in a small frown; concern written all over his face. "Goodnight, Dori." He gave a gentle nod and turned and walked away.

Dori watched him walk back down her street.

I hope you're right.

She wiped a tear from her eye before it escaped to her cheek and walked into the house.

CHAPTER 16

Time dragged on as Dori focused on finals and counted the days between events and time with Mae. She didn't dare tell Mae about the issues she was having with Abigor, she didn't tell anyone. Every event they attended she clung to him desperately hoping to hold onto his affections, even if it was all just for show. Dori was very involved in the events taking place around Winter Solstice, helping plan menus, organize volunteers, decorate, and of course taste test all the best treats, so she kept busy until the big day. Winter Solstice and New Year's were especially important as the more magic that flowed, the better the new year would start. Fairies were definitely superstitious when it came to starting off the year right. If New Year's went well then it symbolized a good and plentiful year.

On the morning of Solstice, Blythe always came into Dori's room extra early as neither one could wait to celebrate, and the two played board games until their parents woke up. This year they were playing an intense game of Sprite Strife, a card game where you collect different types of fairies to build a team and fight against different dark creatures, like goblins and kelpies. But no matter how intense the game got, once they heard their parents' door open up they both jumped up and popped their heads out of Dori's door looking across the hall waiting for the signal. Dori didn't care if she was nearly an adult, Winter Solstice morning would always make her giddy like a little girl.

Their parents sat back sipping their coffee as they watched their kids open up gifts sitting on the floor around the Solstice tree. Now that they were older they got a few gifts from their parents and would get a gift from each sibling. Dori opened some tickets to next summer's Crystal Festival from Blythe and practically tackled him with thankful joy, giving him a big hug. Jareth handed her a small box and she opened it up to see a hot pink plastic crystal cluster. Dori smiled pretending her best that she liked it.

"What, you don't like it?" Jareth questioned.

"No, it's cute," Dori quickly said trying to sound sincere. "Thank you."

"No hug for your big brother?" he asked.

Dori hated hugging Jareth, he made her so uncomfortable, but she leaned in try her best to keep the peace. She gave him a little side hug and thanked everyone for the gifts, as she placed the fake pink crystal back in its box.

"That's it? I got it from the human world since you're so into that," he said staring at the box.

Dori stared, not sure how to answer. It was obviously a cheap souvenir from a gift shop in Delmira, a toy meant for children who cannot be trusted with actual crystals.

"Why don't you ever like anything I get you?" Aggression stained his tone, obviously not happy with Dori's lack of enthusiasm.

"Dori, Jareth, don't start," Cyrus asserted.

Dori's mouth opened in question. Blythe sat there obviously uncomfortable.

"She's the one being a brat!"

"Jareth you heard your father," Adelyn added. "Let's just try and have a nice holiday."

"Whatever," Jareth said standing in a huff and stormed off to his room slamming his door behind him.

The rest of the day went smoothly as Jareth stayed locked away most of the day. Dori and Blythe continued their card game from the morning before they both helped their dad prepare an elaborate breakfast feast for dinner, a Solstice tradition in their home. Abigor had joined her family for dinner briefly and everything seemed perfectly normal; but he left before dessert so the two hadn't gotten to talk much at all. Dori and Blythe helped their dad clean up and after spilling a bowl of winter syrup on himself Blythe went upstairs to go shower.

"So what's the plan for the rest of the day?" Jareth asked, kicking his feet up on the couch, resting them on top of Dori's new plush blanket their mom got her.

"Why don't we watch a movie together," Adelyn suggested with a tender smile.

"As long as Dori doesn't pick, she has the worst taste in movies," Jareth mocked.

"Actually I was gunna go work on some sewing," Dori said from the kitchen as she finished wiping off the table. "I have to finish my New Year's dress," she added, feeling like she needed a genuine excuse to avoid the 'family time'.

"Come on! You've spent all day with Blythe but won't spend a couple hours with me?"

"Like I said, I have to finish my dress before next week," Dori said plainly, turning to walk up the stairs.

"Why don't you ever wanna spend any time with me!" Jareth yelled up the stairs behind her. Dori stopped mid-way up the stairs to have the fight here instead of having him follow her to her room.

"Jareth enough," Cyrus said, coming out of the kitchen and taking a seat on the couch next to Adelyn.

Jareth's eyes glowed red and he started ranting about how Dori always hangs out with Blythe and excludes him from everything. Dori just stood there listening to it all with a vacant look on her face, having heard the same rant time and time again. When he started calling her vulgar names, Cyrus jumped up in a huff, his palms glowing orange with his anger.

"Jareth! I said enough!"

"You always take her side!" Jareth spat out at his father as his hands light with his fury.

"You will not speak to your sister like that," Cyrus began to raise his voice. "Dori, just go upstairs," he said, waving a hand in her direction. "I'm tired of you two always fighting."

Another comment Dori always heard, just standing there listening to Jareth's insults somehow was the *two of them* fighting. She grit her teeth in frustration, slowly taking another step up the stairs.

"We all know she's your favorite, that's why you're trying so hard to give her the internship she doesn't deserve!"

Dori's pride stopped her in her tracks, one more step and she could just walk through the short hallway to her room. She urged herself to escape, *Just keep walking.*

"She has earned her power! Unlike you, she didn't fail out of school, she worked for all she has."

Dori turned around at the top of the stairs thankful for her father's defense of her. Turning just in time to watch a fireball rocket out of Jareth's hand straight at the Solstice Tree. Without hesitation Dori pointed her hand at the tree and quickly pulled it back squeezing her fist tight, consuming the flames and evaporating them out of existence. It was moments like these that made her thankful she continued to practice her Sun fairy magic.

Jareth turned and gave her a dirty look from the bottom of the stairs.

Did you want me to let it burn? Dori thought to herself, her head being much sassier than her voice ever dared to be.

Jareth stormed out the front door, Adelyn calling after him.

"One day where you two aren't at each other's throats!" Cyrus yelled, throwing his hands up that were ablaze with his frustration.

Dori grit her teeth again and finally turned to walk through the hallway. She looked forward to getting out of the house the following day and celebrating Solstice with Mae.

The pair met at Bitter Brew Box and exchanged gifts. Mae had gotten Dori a two banded metal cuff bracelet, that twined together at its center holding a polished black stone.

"It's a hematite stone. I don't know if fairies have the same stone meanings as witches but it symbolizes healing and strength. And the name is derived from the Greek word blood, so big in the vampire community," Mae said to her friend smiling. "I figured it'd be a good reminder of me, my little way of saying you are strong."

"It's beautiful," Dori said placing the bracelet on her wrist admiring the sparkles within the stone. "Thank you," she said meeting Mae's eyes. "Now open yours!"

Mae unwrapped the glittering black wrapping paper to find another layer of different wrapping paper underneath, she rolled her eyes at Dori. She opened up the box to find another box wrapped in the same wrapping paper as the first layer. "What is this?"

Dori laughed, "last layer I promise."

Mae ripped open the paper and the box, pulling out a black snow-globe. Inside was a solid black nutcracker and black glitter swirled around it. Mae's eyes grew wide and she looked from the beautiful thing in her hands to her best friend across from her. "It's stunning," she said turning to shake the glitter around. She held it in her hands elbows propped on the table as Conrad approached with their drinks.

"Wow, cool snow globe," he said placing their cocoas on the table.

"Oh, Conrad, I got you a little something too," Dori said reaching in her bag.

Conrad pulled at the wrapping paper and a t-shirt unfolded in his hands.

"How come he only had one layer?" Mae asked haughtily.

Dori just smiled.

Conrad held up a black t-shirt with a gold design painted on the front, it looked similar to the Bitter Brew Box's logo but in a roaring 20's style layout. "Dude this is sick! Thank you!"

"Wow, great job, Dori," Mae said impressed.

"Thanks! It was actually really fun to design and make," Dori said proud of herself.

"Can you make more so I can sell these?" Conrad asked.

"I don't really have the equipment to do a lot, but maybe one day!" Dori said, taken aback by the question as her cheeks turned red. The designer inside her was jumping with excitement imagining her life doing this professionally.

A few customers walked in and Conrad walked back behind the counter, "Just remember me when you're a famous designer," he said pointing at her.

"No promises," Mae called after him, making Dori laugh.

They both sipped on their cocoa and Dori noticed something missing around Mae's neck. "Hey where's your necklace?"

"Oh the chain broke, I noticed it after I got out of the shower, so I put it in my jewelry box," she said leaning in to whisper, "Don't worry it's safe."

"You promise?" Dori asked with concern.

"Yes, absolutely. So what are we gunna do today?" Mae asked, brushing it off.

"I figured we could just hang here and maybe go through some of Conrad's board games he has stashed in the bookcase," she said, pointing to the loft.

It honestly sounded perfect. With the stressful month Dori had had so far and the extra chaos yesterday Dori was relieved to have a relaxing and peaceful solstice celebration with her best friend, and it made her stress melt away.

CHAPTER 17

Without Abigor to spend time with and not wanting to be home, Dori spent as much of her school break with Mae as she could. Every time they met she felt like she should open up about what Abigor had said to her that night. But she still didn't know how to put it into words, plus Mae didn't care for talking about him anyway so she always just pushed it down. Dori wished she could invite Mae to the New Year's Eve party but New Year's being such a pinnacle in the fairy community they always hosted the party inside Zalor so only fairies would be in attendance.

The castle was adorned with sparkling lights and the features of each wing were glowing with magic. The ivy strewed halls of the Dryad wing were glowing green and bronze, while the Tempes wing was beaming white and blue, with snow falling from the ceiling. With Dori's father being a part of the council, the whole Teresi family would arrive early each year to help set up. Dori had an eye for decorations so she always helped make the castle extra beautiful in preparations while her brothers helped carry in all the food and equipment.

Fairies from all over would flock to the Castle for the New Year's celebration. Many night fairies from Abigor's homeland would be visiting, Tempes fairies from the Arctic, Dryads from the rainforests of South America; every year it was a beautiful gathering of the world of Meltembra. Dori loved how much everyone put aside all differences to celebrate the magic of a new year. Winter Solstice may be her favorite holiday, but New Year's Eve was a close second. Mae had even encouraged her to make her own dress for the occasion this year. Rushing until the last moment, she placed the finishing touches on it moments before her family was out the door.

Looking around at all the lights surrounding the courtyard where all would gather to countdown to the new year and twirled in her sparkling navy blue dress. She shimmered in the evening and her chest lifted with a fresh hopeful breath looking forward to new beginnings. There was still an hour until everyone would arrive, but the bustle of excitement while fairies of every magic readied the castle was a joy that was hard to compare to.

Dori noticed an empty archway and grabbed another string of lights and a ladder. As she reached up to hang the lights the earth shook beneath her and she nearly fell to the ground. She regained her balance, and as soon as she looked up she saw smoke billowing from the eastern part of the city. Dismounting the ladder, she looked up to see a streak of glowing black as a swarm of Night fairies took immediately to the air and rushed to the east side of the island.

She would never forget the cries of fairies filling the sky and the sound of buildings crashing around them.

Fairies from all over the city took flight without hesitation and rushed to the east of the island. Dori flew over Adenike concourse straight toward the Sielu Villa, the most popular hotel in the city. She watched the large trumpet flower column atop of the building drip flames onto the yellow cobblestone walkway below. She flew straight through turning toward the sky, dissipating any flames she could with the wave of her hand. She landed near a fiery crater where a small fountain used to be just outside the entrance to the hotel. At her feet she saw spirit orbs that had fallen from the vines hugging the building, no longer bright shimmering yellow giving sight into the soul, but a burnt crisp of death. She held one in her hands as it lost its integrity and crumbled from a once pure orb into a pile of dust.

Dori heard screams coming from the right, she looked to see fairies running away from a little restaurant tucked in between some perennial homes.

"It's about to blow!" One fairy shouted, urging others to run.

Her body took control of her and she flew directly at the building, landing mere feet away when it blew. She was taken aback by the force of the explosion but flung her arms out encasing the force, not letting it go any further. Tensing her entire body, she slowly tilted like turning a big wheel. Dori's head twitched in her struggle as she dragged her arms through the heavy air, willing the explosion to stop, but the flames went higher. Tears welled in her eyes and sweat appeared on her brow. In the corner of her eye Dori could see a child's room through the window in the home right next door and she wouldn't allow the flames to take it.

Not like the flames that often overtook her home. An anger tingled in her spirit, she forced her hands down, gripping the air tight and gritting her teeth, not taking her eyes off the flames. Her eyes mirrored the flames before her as the roar of the fire lowered, she reached her left arm behind her, slowly lifting it, the weight of the resistance threatened to snap her shoulder. Once her arm was directly behind her, level with her head, she let out a scream and brought it full circle, slamming her hand flat of the warm stones in front of her, dissipating the fire into nothing. Dust flew out, revealing the source of the explosion, what was once a kitchen of the cute little bistro. A chunk of the fountain still sticking out of the stove.

Dori tried to catch her breath, realizing the pain in the left knee from slamming into the ground. Her head pounded and she nearly collapsed from the dizziness overtaking her. A hand touched her shoulder and she flinched pulling back, but quickly relaxed when she saw it was Abigor.

"Are you okay?" He asked helping her up from the ground.

"Yeah," Dori lied, exhaling.

"That was unbel—"

"What's happening?" Dori asked, cutting off his compliment.

"I have no idea, something blew up right in the middle of the square—"

"Help! I need a Meta!" Someone called from across the concourse. Both Abigor and Dori turned toward the call.

"Go, I got this," Abigor said, gesturing toward the bistro.

Dori nodded, and took flight hovering just above the ground moving as quickly as she could, back over the crater toward a little pond under a blue blossom tree. A Fauna fairy was holding the hand of a Water fairy laying on the ground, a large shard of glass was lodged in her side. Dori tried to hold in her gasp at the old woman laying at the edge of the pond, one hand draped in the water, her eyes fixed on the ripples on the surface as the purple berries fell from the blossom tree above.

"Please. Do you have healing powers? I can't help her," the small fairy said, with terror staining in his pink eyes.

Dori squatted down, grabbing the older fairy's hand from his. "I'll do what I can, go see if you can help at the bistro across the way," Dori pointed a hand over to where Abigor was helping bandage someone's leg.

Kneeling down beside the frail woman, Dori waved a hand over the wound, she could sense the intensity, the fairy was already dying. The blood spilled from her side, turning the pure blue pond to a death-stained shade of purple. Dori knew there was no healing her, so she did what she could to absorb the pain.

She closed her eyes and yellow sparkles danced between her fingers as she waved her hands over the large wound in the fairy's side. Mouth wide opened she let out a silent cry, holding her breathe. She felt the pain enter her own body, and the fairy turned her face to look at Dori.

"The pain—it's gone," the old fairy let out with a small smile, that lasted barely a second as the life left her face and her head fell limp in Dori's lap. Dori held the woman's hand tight to her chest as she watched the bright teal of her eyes fade to grey, her pale blue hair still dancing in the wind. The pain Dori had absorbed left her body, she wanted to feel relief but she only felt the emptiness of the stranger's body she held in her arms. Dori sunk back on her heels; her dress now coated in dirt, had lost all it's sparkle.

Through tear filled eyes she looked up at the villa, orbs still falling from its face. The Sielu Villa was a haven for fairies of all kinds, welcoming visitors from all over Meltembra. With easy access to Lithos Ridge it was nearly as sacred, the spirit orbs covering the building gave the entire villa a powerful aura, nurturing all who visited. It was the biggest Meta fairy area in the city. A tear rolled through the soot on Dori's cheek as she watched Sun and Water fairies flying all around putting out the remainder of the flames. A long banner fell to the ground with a crisp "2013" curling into the burnt edges of the New Year decoration. Dori looked to the entrance and saw her little brother helping a child out of the building. The level above weakened by the fire the Water fairies had already put out. The scream barely left her mouth as Blythe looked up to see the arches above coming down toward him.

CHAPTER 18

Awakening from her nightmare screaming her brother's name. Her brain was replaying every moment from that horrible night. Her brother ran into her room having heard her cries. Dori looked at him through tear filled eyes.

"It's okay, I'm here," Blythe said sitting down in his sister's arms.

"The building, it was falling on you," Dori whimpered hugging him close.

"I know," Blythe choked out. "But you saved us, I'm right here."

Dori had been extremely weakened in the moment, but it was in her nature to protect her brother. She didn't know how but when she lifted her hands intending to simply stop the massive piece of building from falling on her brother it had turned to bubbles and floated away. Despite having just been rescued from a burning building the small child with Blythe was smiling, jumping up to pop the bubbles. Dori replayed it in her head over and over but she still couldn't figure it out. All she was thinking about was her little brother and not wanting to lose him. She didn't even remember anything after that. The last moment she recalled was collapsing and someone catching her. When she woke hours later, she found out it was Abigor who had caught her and brought her home that night.

Dori held Blythe close and they both fell back asleep clinging to one another.

School was still out as the city attempted to recover from the bombings. Dori had seen Abigor briefly the day after, but he was busy working with the task force to find answers about the attack. Today was the first day Dori actually had a breather, having been volunteering all week as a healer and helping serve food at the makeshift shelter set up in the castle.

As she walked through the door of Bitter Brew Box, her brain tormented her with the view of the flames surrounding her. She had never flown so fast in her entire life or used so much of her fire abilities, the fires she had experience with at her house were nothing in comparison to entire streets going up in flames. She tried to shake the memories from her head as she greeted Mae with a hug.

"Hey, how are you doing?" Mae asked. Mae had called on New Year's Day to wish Dori a happy new year and Dori was only able to stay on for a few moments as she was busy helping patients in the infirmary. Mae was astonished at the news and waited eagerly by her phone all week for updates from her friend, wishing she herself could be there helping with the aftermath.

"Not getting much sleep but happy to be away from all of it for a bit. Things have calmed down a bit, they've started laying out plans for a big memorial service and rebuilding plans," Dori said.

"I'm so sorry, this is all so horrible. No news from Abigor yet on the attackers?"

"No, we haven't talked much. And my dad's been so busy I haven't got the slightest idea where they are on the investigation," Dori said trying to wrap her head around the whole thing. "But I don't want to think about that right now, I just need to clear my head."

"Oh, of course," Mae said grabbed her friend's hand. "Iced mochas and a jam sesh in the loft?"

Dori looked at her friend starting to tear up, "Sounds perfect," she whispered.

Laughter and dancing lasted about 5 minutes before Dori broke down, happy to have a friend she didn't have to be brave for. To have a place where she could melt down and not pretend to be okay. She wasn't okay, and she hated acting like she was. Mae held Dori in a hug until she worked through her tears. Then she sat and listened to the horrifying stories of Dori's experiences from that night.

A horrifying thought popped into Mae's head, what if Dori's professor had been right. What if there was a sect of fairies that was prepared to destroy everything, that would be looking for Dori because of her power. Mae opened her mouth to mention it but her whimpering friend in front of her was scared enough as it is. She bit her tongue and swore to herself she would do everything in her power to protect Dori. She would stay alert and ask her own questions about what happened in Zalor that night. If there was someone after her best friend she would find them, before they found her. And they would pay for all the pain they have caused her.

"Dori, you didn't mention if you had gotten hurt. I know you can heal but did you get hurt at all?" Mae asked her friend concerned.

"It was all kind of crazy, I got a few scratches and bruises but I am mostly okay. My abdominal pain is worse though, I don't know if it is because of all the chaos of the night or what, but it's been pretty bad," Dori said touching her side.

"You've mentioned your pain before, but you said you're healing abilities don't effect it for long right?"

"Yeah it makes a difference on the surface but doesn't really help with the pain." Dori lifted her shirt slightly to reveal the bruise looking marks on her body. Mae was alarmed by the amount of bruising on her friends sides, she looked as if she had been beaten. Mae had seen injuries like this before but with vampire blood running through her system she could easily heal a person if she wanted. She wasn't sure how it would work on a fairy, especially since that fairy had the ability to heal herself. As Dori went to pull her shirt bad down Mae saw a flicker of red specks throughout the bruising.

"Hold on a sec," Mae said moving in closer to take a better look. Mae knew blood trauma, she knew it well.

But the marks on her friend's abdomen were unlike anything she had ever seen before. "Dori why would there be bright red marks in this bruising?"

Dori looked down, "Oh, I don't know. I've never really looked that hard at it."

"How long have you had this?"

"It started a couple years ago," Dori answered saddened at the thought of how long she's been suffering. "I was perfectly fine, then just collapsed in pain. I went to healers and my mom even brought me to some physicians outside of Meltembra. But they all say there's physically nothing wrong with me."

Mae looked at her friend, having been through something similar herself before she was turned, she knew the pain she was enduring was nothing compared to the torment of not knowing, and not being able to trust your own body.

"It's never been this bad though, it's gotten worse these last couple weeks," Dori said.

"Wait, it was getting worse before the bombing?"

"Yeah, it kinda started after Abigor told me—" Dori stopped short realizing she never told Mae about what

Abigor had said to her that night at the beginning of December. She hadn't told anyone.

Mae leaned in looking ready to pounce. "Dori, what did he do?"

Dori looked at Mae, the beautiful, strong girl she had always been able to be honest with, especially since telling her she was a fairy. But Mae already didn't like Abigor and Dori didn't want to hear the inevitable 'leave him' that would no doubt come from her mouth the instant she told her the awful things Abigor said to her. "Nothing, it was just a bad fight and it's long over with now after everything," Dori said. It hurt her to be dishonest, but it was better this way. No need to make her best friend dislike her boyfriend more if they could work through this issue. The thoughts of *if* roared in her mind, tormenting her. She began to fidget trying not to cry on the spot or let her face reveal how hard she was trying to hold back tears.

Mae could see how torn Dori was, she knew there was more to it but it had already been a trying day. She would look further into the fairy books Dori lent her and focus on her injury, she would think of several ways to kill Abigor later. It would be a nice way to pass the time while Dori went to the memorial the next day.

Sitting perfectly lifeless in her black velvet dress, Dori sat with the other council family members to the side of a large stage set up for the occasion. Sitting between each of her brothers; Blythe barely taking his eyes off the floor, and Jareth constantly fidgeting and mumbling obscene things under his breath, she was more anxious about what Jareth might do, than she was sad about the memorial.

Normally looking at the people of Zalor was like looking into a kaleidoscope, colors bright and dark cascading over the lot, but that was not the case today. Every last fairy was dressed in dark colors, black for the traditional funeral look, and then there were those dressed in red, standing out, making the statement they intended to. In Meltembra red was the color of dark magic, it symbolized many things but it's mainly symbolized the blood spilt when meddling with dark magic.

There had been a lot of talk about the bombing being from dark magic, whether rumors of the magic itself fighting back, a cult of dark magic users resurfacing and causing this mayhem, or even the outlandish discussions of Dahlia's potential return to enact vengeance. Yes, those wearing red were here to speak out against the darkness of what had taken place, meant to loudly exclaim the evil at hand. Of course no one was happy about what had happened, and it was indeed an act of war, but many fairies within the realm believed it was an act of defiance against the council's recent efforts to further ostracize the lost fae, not some great darkness.

The high school choir sang a beautiful ballad of the Prayer for Peace, a traditional fae song for the dead. Family members of the fallen spoke, each fairy was honored with a spark of their magic color lit in the sky as their family members were presented with flowers. Then Asteria Lekatai took the stage, the Elder of the Night fairies. She wore a long high necked black dress, with a crescent moon cut out just below her neck outlined in navy blue gems. The gems sprinkled throughout the dress glistened in the daylight as the long train elegantly traced over the steps as she took her place at the large podium.

Asteria stood tall at the podium, eyeing the crowd before she began to speak. The 500 year old Night fairy was extremely intimidating, not normally one to be asked to speak at an event as sensitive as this one, but she would close out the memorial with mention of what the warriors plan was moving forward from the brutal attack.

"Good evening, Zalor," Asteria began in a somber tone. She needed no introduction, every citizen of Meltembra knew who the Council members were. "Thank you all for being here and the tributes you have paid to our fallen fairies. This atrocious attack has taken much from us, but we are a force much stronger than the waves that beat against us." Asteria took a long pause surveying the masses. "As we grieve, we must also grow stronger, for we have a greater battle ahead. The Night fairies and I have discovered the parties responsible for the bombing." Hundreds of thousands of fairies sat completely still, it was incredible how silent the city was. "We are still investigating exactly how they were able to enter our borders, but we have discovered that the Seraphina Witches and their Vampires were behind the attack."

The silence broke immediately and everyone was in a fuss over the news. Dori could have been the only one not talking with those who sat beside her. None of it made any sense, only fairies could enter the borders of Meltembra, it was impossible for the Seraphina or vampires to enter their realm. Dori's mind was racing but kept circling back to Mae, she didn't know what this meant for her friend.

Asteria put her hand up to quiet the crowd. "I understand you all will have many questions and the warriors in your villages will do their best to answer those questions. We intend to keep our investigation open to the public and will keep you as up to date as possible. For now, we need your cooperation in our new curfew and restrictions." You could practically hear the younger fairies roar at the idea. "Further information will be sent to your homes. The barrier is being closed as we speak." Mayhem spread across the crowd, but Asteria continued on, head held high. "The Faebana will be the only way into Zalor, the council understands many of you operate with businesses in Delmira, permits to utilize the Faebana will be handed out following the service at Elandvor. Please bring proper documentation. The most crucial thing right now, is that no one must approach the east of the island, and absolutely no fraternizing with the east islanders. As we gather further information and plan our next course of action, it is of the utmost importance that any fairies permitted in Delmira keep a safe distance from Cano Valley and its residents as best they can."

Dori swallowed hard. The crowd started to blur together, unable to focus she sat there in a daze as her brain filled with the thought of her best friend. Trusting Mae to be there for her during her most painful moments had been a huge relief these past days. It was a comfort to have someone she didn't have to put up a front for, the first time she had ever had that in her life. The possibility that Mae was somehow linked to this tragedy made her wonder if life was simply playing a cruel joke on her. Dori got nauseous the more she thought about it.

Blinking hard, pulling herself out of the daze, the crowd came back into focus and she turned to Blythe sitting next to her. She refused to turn to her left and listen to Jareth mumble about the vermin we allow to live on our once sacred island. Seeing fear rise in Blythe's face, she grabbed for his hand and gave a small reassuring smile. She felt tension release ever so slightly and it was a happy distraction from thinking of Mae. Dori had to see her. But as she was trying to think of how, Asteria continued to explain that warrior fairies were coming from all over to stay for the next several months. More than that, Water and Tempes fairies would be coming from the city of Sororia and a fire sect of Sun fairies coming from Nyaloa.

"The council has a plan, that we will discuss further with the leaders from Sororia and Nyaloa upon their arrival. These next months we must come together, no matter our kin, and trust in the council," Asteria said, standing tall above the city. "We will recover and continue on better than ever before."

Dori looked at her father as his face fell, as adjudicate he would be privy to the information Asteria was being so vague about. And he did not look like he was proud of the plan the council had ahead. Swallowing hard, terror rose within her.

She needed to see Mae, tonight.

CHAPTER 19

Tearing apart her room, cursing under her breath, Mae normally tried to stay quiet in her room to not draw attention but she didn't care. She had opened her jewelry box to finally fix the chain on her necklace so she could get back out in the day, but it was missing. She knew exactly where she placed it after discovering it was broken. Mae's face began to contort with anger, her eyes turned red as she looked up through furrowed brow. As if on cue, her mother walked in her room asking what was going on.

Mae jolted 180° to face her mother. "Has anyone been in my room? I'm missing something very important," Mae said accusingly.

"Mae..." her mother said taking a seat on her bed. "We knew you wouldn't agree."

Mae was caught off guard. But she should've suspected it was no accident her necklace from her fairy friend was missing. "Wouldn't agree to what mother? Where is my necklace?" Mae practically spat at her mother.

"You couldn't really think that you could be friends with one of them and Zagan not find out?" Mae's eyes grew wider as her mother's fell. "But—"

"But your little friendship proved helpful," Mae's father interrupted, appearing in her doorway, dangling her chain in his hand.

Mae flashed across the room and snatched the necklace out of his hand, "Give that back!" She hissed. She held up the pendant and saw the stone inside was missing. "What did you do?" She asked eyes burning red and fangs dropping from behind her upper lip in her anger.

"The witches needed fae magic to open the barrier," her mother said quietly behind her. "The stone withered away as they drained the magic held within."

"For the first time in centuries we have the upper hand, Zagan is most proud of your work," her father grinned.

Mae ignored her father's condescension turning to her mother, "you mean to tell me the attack was—"

"All thanks to you, daughter," her father answered proudly.

The air left her lungs. She couldn't grasp the air around her. Falling to the floor she looked at the empty pendant in her hand. Quivering as she finally took short breaths in.

"Pick yourself up, child, we have merely come ahead in this war, there is still work to be done," her father said patting her on the shoulder before vanishing.

Mae looked up through tear filled eyes at her mother, "How could you be a part of this?"

Her mother stood, "The fairies have become arrogant in their reign on this island. As your father said, we finally have the upper hand. They now have reason to fear us, and Zagan believes we can keep things quiet for some time while they recover, preserving the lives of our own."

"Since when do you take orders from Zagan?" Mae sneered.

"You forget I was once one of those witches the fairies despise. I will not apologize for helping them regain power that was stolen from them," Mae's mother said proudly looking down her nose at her on the floor. "Grieve your friendship and move on," she said before vanishing from Mae's room.

Mae slumped further into the floor gripping the necklace in hand. Her anger faded and turned to sorrow, as she began to weep she could feel the aura of the necklace. Holding the pendant in the middle of her open palms, she uttered the words "Vide Aspectum", as she curled her fingers around the necklace and closed her eyes. Head tilted to the ceiling, the memory came into sight. Mae looked around at the dark stone walls, questioning where she was, when she saw a large pit of bright orange. She barely had time to take in the fact she was inside the volcano, when her eyes bore the sight of two fairies floating above the pit of lava. To the left a collection of witches stood on the overhang of the plateau, Mae watched like a fly on the dark cavern wall. Avyanna stood at the helm of the cliff, and with one swift movement she sliced the necks of both fairies from 10 feet away. Without a sound both fairies fell into the pit, instantly catching fire. The flames absorbed their bodies as they slowly sank lower into the pit.

"Do you have the final key?" Avyanna asked one of the witches behind her.

Mae watched her necklace dangle from the witch's hand, urging herself to move forward, she could do nothing but watch as it was handed to the dark witch. Avyanna whispered something into her hands as she clutched the necklace. Opening her palms the necklace rose from her hands and moved slowly to the center of cavern.

"With me now, sisters," Avyanna called, reaching out her arms to either side, summoning a chorus of chants.

Bursts of light shot from the pendant of her necklace and circle around it; a luminous sphere of purple so bright it lit the entire dark cavern. Avyanna shouted something and the sphere shot out stripes of purple glitter in every direction then dropped into the pit. For a moment, in the soft glow of the lava Mae saw the remaining necklace floating above the pit, the pendant melted into itself, dripping into the lava below. Swiftly, she was transported back to her room, opening her eyes as the tears began to fall.

Mae knew this could only get worse. It was well known the fairies had been here forever but all the research she had done recently showed her that this island wasn't just their home, but a sacred place long before witches even existed. The Seraphina and the Vampires were the ones who claimed what was not theirs. The sheer amount of fairies that dwelt within the mountains could easily wipe their village out, and now they had a completely valid reason to want to be rid of the lot of them. Mae dreaded what would come next, but more so, she dreaded the part she had played in it, and knowing she would have to tell her best friend. A black fog of loneliness overcame her, she sat lifeless clutching the necklace as if it was the hope her friend wouldn't say goodbye.

With the sun down they could've met anywhere, but Dori had texted Mae saying she needed to meet at Bitter Brew and only had a short window before she needed to be back home. Pacing back and forth on the loft awaiting the arrival of her friend, there was a pit in Mae's stomach unwilling to let up for even a moment. The cafe was silent, having closed hours earlier, only the sound of Conrad placing chairs up on the tables. She heard footsteps come from below the loft, and Dori appeared from the back of the café. Usually she would rush down and greet her best friend with a hug, but today she couldn't get her feet to budge. She just stared down from the loft.

"Hey Conrad," Dori said, somberly walking past the coffee bar.

"Hey gorgeous," he said simply while cleaning off the bar, making her smile ever so slightly.

As she watched Dori approach the loft, Mae still couldn't get herself to move to greet her, the shame weighing heavy on her. They sat in comfy arm chairs across from one another, silently for some time, then Dori told Mae about the service, about the beautiful tribute to the fallen fairies, the valor awards many received, and the announcement of rebuilding plans.

"Then the Night fairy Elder took the stage to discuss the attack," Dori said looking down at her feet.

Mae swallowed hard, *she knows.*

"They are still trying to figure out the details of how but," Dori paused looking up at her vampire friend tears threatening to burst from her eyes. "Mae, they say it was the Seraphina and Zagan."

Mae looked at her friend filled with shame. "I know," she whispered.

Dori was taken aback, startled to look at her friend shaking her head in confusion. "What do you mean you know?"

"I just found out too," Mae reassured her friend thinking of how it must've sounded. "My dad––" Mae broke off breaking eye contact.

Staring at Mae, fear filling her soul. "Mae? You know how they broke the barrier?"

Mae looked up with tear filled eyes. Chewing on her bottom lip she held up the necklace. Dori was quiet looking at the missing pendant. "I'm not sure how, but I guess they were able to extract the fairy magic from the pendant. They cast some kind of spell to be able to put the... the bomb, in your world," Mae sniffled.

Dori was breathless, filled with shame and then the briefest moment of anger. "How did they get it?"

"Remember it had broken? Which now I'm thinking was no accident. I had it in my jewelry box in my room and my mom, or my dad, I'm not sure which one, went into my room and took it," Mae said, frustrated at her parents. "Dori I am *so* sorry."

"I asked you if it was safe," Dori whispered aggressively. "You *promised* me it was safe," her voice rising with each word.

"I know I didn't think—"

"No! You didn't!" Dori snapped. "Mae, I told you when I gave you that necklace the risk I took for you!" Dori jumped out of her chair tears spilling from her eyes, pacing back at forth. "I trusted you!" Dori screamed, her eyes flashing a red glare. Mae jerked her head back in surprise, having never seen her friend angry. "With my magic!" Dori added pointing a hand to herself, as her eyes swelled with tears. She gasped trying to catch her breath, turning away from Mae, the air shook as it left her. "It's all my fault, mine," her voice broke muddled with shame.

Mae stood and approached her friend now standing on the other edge of the loft, "What do you mean it's your fault?"

"I made the necklace," Dori spat in anger, jaw clenched tight. "I handed over fairy magic to a *vampire*," she said, looking over her shoulder at Mae. The word 'vampire' staining the air between them.

Mae was a little insulted, "You were helping me, your friend. It should've never been used for such a thing," Mae said, reaching out to Dori.

Dori pulled away from Mae's reach and turned in a huff, "Exactly! *My* friend! I wasn't thinking about anyone else and what it could mean sending a powerful gem filled with my magic into your village!" Dori was hysterical.

"Dori, this isn't your fault!" Mae stood, grabbing her friends arms, trying to bring her back to reality.

"Mae," Dori said seriously looking her straight in the eyes. "It was *my* magic," Dori turned in a daze. "My magic, tainted with all that blood," she whimpered collapsing into the loft railing behind her.

"Dori, listen to me. This was a terrible thing but you are not responsible for what happened," Mae said kneeling in front of her.

"It was *our* friendship," she said in a faded scream that bled shame.

Mae looked at her startled again.

"If we weren't friends they wouldn't have taken the magic, wouldn't have been able to break the barrier," she was getting hysterical again. "And all those fairies would still be alive," Dori said putting her face in her hands. "I can't see you anymore, Mae."

"What?" Mae knew she wouldn't react well but never expected her to blame herself, maybe that she would be angry with her but she didn't understand what was happening.

"I shouldn't even be here now, I came to tell you the fairies are demanding us to stay in the realm, to not associate with the witches or vampires," Dori muttered, slowly taking her face from her palms. "They are closing the barrier, no one in or out," she added staring at Mae with numb eyes. "I was only able to get here through my closet portal. But once the barrier is fully up there will be no way into Delmira."

"For how long?"

"I don't know," she said finally picking herself off the floor. "But maybe it's better this way," Dori approached the stairs not looking Mae in the eyes.

Mae jolted up. "You can't honestly believe that," she said following her down the winding staircase.

"Of course not Mae," Dori said turning around on the stairs. "You are possibly the best friend I have ever had, but I can't risk the safety of my people. This whole thing is MY FAULT!" she pleaded as tears streaked down her cheeks.

"No it's not," Mae said with a stern look on her face.

"You don't get it," Dori said, beginning her descent down the stairs again.

"Then explain it to me!" Mae yelled after her.

"I went against my people when I made you that necklace, I knew I could get in trouble but I did it anyway and this is what came of it!" Dori yelled back, heading for the door to the bathroom, where she had once cast her closet charm to grab blankets on a cozy night they spent in the loft.

Mae rushed around her and cut her off from the door. "You did it because we matter to each other. I am not going to let you blame this on yourself the same way you blame yourself for everything," she said staring her down.

"Mae, this is different than anything else. And I shouldn't have even come to meet with you, if anyone found out what I did," Dori gulped. "Well... I don't know what they would do."

Mae grabbed Dori's face to look at her. "Dori, you cannot blame yourself, what happened was awful but it is in no way your fault."

But Dori was eyes showed nothing but numbness, she shook her head from Mae's grasp. "I'm sorry, I can't. I have to go."

Pushing past her, Mae called after her best friend as she walked through the door, but couldn't convince herself to follow. She was too used to this moment, watching people she cared for walk out of her life, she had no will to fight it.

"You're not going after her?" Conrad appeared from the back room.

"Leave it alone, Conrad," Mae said frustrated.

"Mae this isn't either of your faults, you need to make sure she knows that," Conrad pleaded gesturing back toward the door.

Mae looked at the door hoping Dori would walk back through. She shook her head, "I tried but she won't listen. Her mind is made up, if she's done then so am I," she lied trying to convince herself.

"Mae," Conrad took a long pause waiting for her to look at him. "She's your best friend. She's broken right now, you need to be there."

Mae pushed the bathroom door open, but there was no closet. Not even a sparkle left behind. She stared at the black tiles and wood trim along the wall. It was just a bathroom, devoid of any magic. She walked to the wall where Dori had cast her closet charm, she loved watching her friend do her magic. Mae fell to the floor, hand pressed to the wall.

"I'll be here when you get back Dori. I'll always be here," she sobbed to herself.

CHAPTER 20

School opened back up the first week of February, Dori was happy to have something to do to get her out of the house but walking into Professor Lenora's class, she knew it was not going to be a pleasant day. Lenora barely looked at her all class and Dori didn't dare move after class ended. Once the last student walked out the door and silence laid over the classroom Lenora put a hand up and added a barrier to her classroom door, not looking up from the papers she was fiddling with on her desk. Dori sank a little lower in her seat.

"Don't worry, the council believes the magic was absorbed from living fairies that were taken months ago," Lenora said softly, still locked to the papers in front of her. "Which I believe in part— is true, as I understand there was some sort of blood sacrifice required to access the magic in your stone."

Dori opened her mouth but her voice froze when Lenora picked her face up and locked eyes with her.

"I warned you how dangerous this magic can be."

"I know, I—"

"You risked everything!" Lenora burst from her chair and slammed her hands on her desk. Dori squinted and pulled her gaze down in shame. Lenora sighed heavily and spoke softly again, "Endora, this magic," she paused, her face twitching in frustration. "You needed to keep it safe," Lenora said crisply.

"I'm sorry," Dori said, face locked on the desk in front of her, her lip quivering.

"I should be done with you! Done with the lessons," Lenora said, raising her voice and punching her words into the air. "This *foolishness* is unforgivable," Lenora exhaled aggressively.

Dori tightened her eyes, not caring if she cried. This shame was too heavy to bare.

"Look at me, child," she said, pulling her voice back down but remaining stern.

Dori slowly picked her head up. "I didn't—"

"I know," Lenora interrupted. "But you cannot play with this magic. It has been lost for centuries, *snuffed out*! Because of the power it possesses." Lenora rolled her shoulders back standing tall, taking a deep breath. "It has been lying in wait to be awakened again. And it chose you." Lenora looked at Dori peering into her very soul.

Dori stared up at Lenora, her eyes screaming the question *Why me?*

"You are so much stronger than you know. And a part of something much bigger than this war with the vampires."

"I don't understand, you have Alchemy magic too. How could I possibly have awoken this magic?"

"I possess Alchemy magic, yes," Lenora said, moving in and grabbing Dori's arms. "But Endora, you are an Alchemy *fairy!* You will be ten times the fairy I could ever be," she spoke slowly letting the words hang between them, giving her arms a squeeze.

Dori looked at the woman before her. Annonette Lenora, the Meta fairy that was begged by the council year after year to take her place among them, even after centuries of refusing them they still came to her for advice. She was possibly the most powerful fairy of this age, and somehow she believed frail little, screw-up

Dori would be more powerful than her. Dori's tears finally broke the surface.

"Lost magics are lost, not because no one possesses them, but because their power has dwindled to practically nothing. Alchemy naturally flows through you, you discovered it all on your own. You have the potential to bring it to life again," Lenora continued finally releasing Dori's arms.

"But, I'm just—me," Dori muttered.

"You are exactly who you are supposed to be." Lenora looked at Dori endearingly, letting the moment sit for a minute. "I trust you are no longer in communication with your friend," Lenora spoke with empty tone.

Dori looked down again with guilt. "No, we haven't spoken since the night of the memorial."

"Endora," Lenora said, compelling Dori to lift her head again. "I will express again the *utmost* importance of our secret," the word lingering on her lips, as she lifted her chin high.

"I won't tell a soul," Dori said in the most serious tone she could muster as her throat still burned with the tears cursing her eyes.

Lenora wrote Dori an excuse pass to give to her next professor and released the barrier from the door without another word. Dori walked down the hall pulling at her eyes to hide the fact she had been crying, when she saw her boyfriend across the corridor.

"Hey babe, I was just coming to find you," Abigor said sweetly, approaching her.

"What are you doing here?" she uttered trying to hide her face.

"Bringing a couple NWTC students back that were trying to skip class, figured I would say hi while I was here," he said finally reaching her and kissing her a kiss on the cheek.

"Oh." Dori was surprised at his affections, they hadn't seen really seen each other since New Year's, they had each reached out a couple times to check in, but this was the first they'd really seen each other since then.

"Are you okay? You seem upset," Abigor said, touching her arm tenderly.

Dori looked down at his hand, "Yeah, just first day back and stuff," she gave a small unconvincing smile.

"You were with Professor Lenora right? Is she helping ready you for the internship?"

"No just TA stuff, preparing stuff for the semester," Dori uttered, looking back up at him questioning his sudden interest.

"Right, probably not much else to prepare for the internship, I'm sure you'll get it," Abigor said smiling, running his hands through the ends of her hair, looking intently at the violet waves. "I'll walk you to your next class."

They walked through the corridor and down the glittering sapphire hall in the Water Wing where her Creativity in Magic class was held.

"How have you been?" Dori asked, not sure how to question his attitude toward her today.

"Things have been rough, lots of work rebuilding, and training harder then ever, but," he paused stopping them both in their tracks and pulling her to look at him. "I'm thankful I have someone as strong as you looking out for me."

Dori stood there silent, searching his face for understanding.

"I know I've been caught up in warrior duty the last month, but I've really missed you," he said, pulling her in for a hug.

Dori melted at his touch, focusing intently on not letting the tears creep up again.

"I don't want to keep you from class, I'll talk to you later," he said, giving her another kiss on the cheek.

Dori stood for a moment watching Abigor walk back through the hall. Her head hurt from crying earlier and she didn't have the energy to process the confusion filling her brain. She gulped down her feelings, flinching as a jolt pierced her side, and she walked into her class.

CHAPTER 21

Dori tossed and turned in her bed; seeing images of fairies under rubble, hearing the screams and cries. Jareth approached her, offering a hand to help her up from the ashes she sat in. But his grip on her wrist changed from helpful to aggressive, and he threw her back down again. The dust coming up into her face and choking her. Dori knew she was dreaming, she fought to wake up but she couldn't escape the cruelty of her mind. Her nightmares often twisted her fears and traumas together, as if reality wasn't enough torture. Jareth screamed at her, kicking her in the side. Dori twitched, yearning to wake up, to escape the torment.

Sitting up hyperventilating, she grabbed the ache in her side as a tear crept its way to the surface of her eyes, waking her dog that was laying at her feet. The fuzzy bronze creature approached her and sat in her lap, sniffing her face. Dori gave her a hug as the tear finally escaped and rolled down her cheek, her dog licking it away with her large blue tongue. After sitting for several minutes she finally got out of bed, wincing at the pain in her side, and walked into the little bathroom to get ready for the day. Dori aggressively washed her face trying to scrub away the dread staining her soul. Water dripped from her cheeks as she blankly stared into the mirror, the eyes of sorrow staring back at her.

"Happy freaking birthday, Dor," she said.

As she dried her face the door swung open nearly hitting her.

"Morning," Jareth said, giving a quick smile as he grabbed his toothbrush.

"You can't knock?"

"What's the big deal? It's just me," Jareth scoffed.

Dori just blinked, turning to the side trying to hide her hostility in her "excuse me," as she squeezed past him out of the bathroom. Blythe met her in the hall and gave her a big hug.

"Happy Birthday, Dor!" Blythe yelled excitedly as he squeezed her tight.

Dori's joy was momentary as Jareth called out from the bathroom, "Oh yeah it's your birthday! What are we doing today?"

Dori rolled her eyes as her younger brother released his hug, giving her a wide-eyed stare that made her smile. Then the smell of sweet cinnamon hit her nose. Walking downstairs into the kitchen Dori's father greeted her.

"Happy Birthday, beautiful," Cyrus said, giving her a kiss on the forehead. "I made your favorite, Fae Toast with sugar dust. And I picked up blue sap caramel too."

"Thanks, Dad," Dori said, tearing up a bit at the gesture.

"Wow! Sweet," Jareth said, pushing Dori aside to serve himself first.

"I know we just planned for birthday dinner tonight but the weather has turned a bit and I was thinking we could do the crystal trail," Cyrus suggested.

"Uggghhh a hike?" Jareth grunted as he shoved a forkful of the fae toast in his mouth. "Sounds like an awful way to spend a Saturday," he said smacking his syrupy lips.

"Well, you don't have to go with," Blythe said as he handed Dori a plate with extra whipped cream and blue caramel, she smiled in thanks.

Dori picked at her breakfast, thinking of Mae, who would probably collapse just walking in her house right now with the cinnamon filled air. Cyrus kept topics on the lighter side as the four enjoyed their breakfast. He had brought a plate up to Adelyn, who was having a rough morning and only had gotten up to say goodbye and just before leaving for the hike, handing Dori a glittery birthday card and giving her a kiss on the cheek.

Dori, Blythe, and their dad flew up north landing at the base of Mount Celeste, just north of Elandvor. The side of the teal mountain had a path lined with crystals of all kinds on either side, shining pink rhodonite, glowing yellow citrine, deep blue sapphire, blood red jasper. Dori smiled in anticipation for the beauty that lie ahead, the path outside was nothing compared to the wonders inside the mountain. The trail coiled through the mountain, with no regard for such trivialities as gravity. Crystalized walls encased the trail, opening into caverns in the mountain, with large stalactites of crystals hanging suspended from the cavern ceilings. A glowing teal creek carved it's way through the mountain twisting all around. It was early enough in the season that barely anyone else was on the trail, Dori revelled in the time with her father and brother, trying not to dread the awkward family dinner that would conclude her birthday celebration. For a moment she was able to forget how sad she was, her pain even lifted ever so slightly.

The remainder of the day was better than she had anticipated. Abigor joined them for dinner and kept Jareth distracted with all his stories. To Dori's surprise Abigor had gotten her the newest book from her favorite author and a shimmering purple mug to add to her collection. The thoughtfulness of his gift and the way he held her hand during dessert made her insides tickle again. Since the bombing they rarely got to spend any time together, but they stole moments together when they could. Even with the minimum time, they were able to rely on each other in the past couple months after the bombing, and she was hopeful that the worst was behind them.

Dori sat on the curb outside her home pondering the day, overthinking her life, feeling like it was as stagnant as her age now that she was 18 and would age much slower. Hunched over her knees, she twirled her fingers through the blades of grass. Her eyes lost focus as a fog crept over her thoughts.

Flames. Nothing but flames. Tightening of her throat, Dori tried to gasp for air—

A friendly voice breaks through the fog of her mind. "Happy birthday, Dori."

Dori picked her head up to see Sage approaching, she gave a small thank you.

Sage took a seat next to her, "Hold out your hands."

Dori sat up and put her hands out in front of her, leaning her wrists on her knees. Sage dropped a tiny brown seed in her hands, Dori cocked her head looking at the dot in her hands. Sage leaned in and waved her fingers elegantly in the air above Dori's hands, forest green sparkles rained from her fingers and the seed broke open. Dori watched as a large sparkling chrysanthemum slowly formed from the seed, it's indigo petals spread in her palms until the flower completely covered her hands. Her favorite type of flower.

"Thank you," Dori said, looking up from the flower to give her friend a teary-eyed smile.

"Curse of the birthday again?" Sage asked, locking her olive eyes with the tears welling in Dori's. Dori always had the worst luck around her birthday, every year without fail something would happen that would ruin the celebration. For years her and Sage joked that she must've been born on a cursed day of some sort. Even if she was able to make it through the day unscathed it was only a matter of time until the curse popped up stealing her happiness again.

"Actually it was fine," Dori shrugged looking back at the flower. "My dad made fae toast, we hiked the Crystal trail, had a nice dinner," Dori said plainly. As if on cue shouting broke out in the house, both Dori and Sage turned toward the noise.

"So you're sitting out here to avoid that?"

Dori contemplated going in, but Blythe was out with friends and her dad was home, she'd let him handle whatever fit Jareth was throwing. "No, I'm just..." Dori trailed off, stuck in her sadness. "I wanted to spend time with my one friend and can't."

"Your human friend right? But since the barrier closed you can't."

Dori just nodded.

"I'm sorry, I know you guys have gotten really close, it sucks you can't hang out right now," Sage said, placing a hand on Dori's back. Dori looked over at her and gave her a genuine smile, appreciating her friend's empathy.

The sky cracked above them and both girls looked to the sky as the rain began to fall.

Sage's cheeks squished up as she looked ecstatically at the sky then back down at Dori. "A birthday gift from the sky."

Dori's sadness melted as the smell of spring rain consumed her, shutting off her thoughts. She jumped up, grabbing Sage's hands lifting her off the curb. The two danced barefoot in the street, soaking in the warmth of the new season.

Spring flowers unfurled across the island, painting the air with warmth. It had been over three months since that moment at the café. Dori resumed her studies with Professor Lenora at school, grateful to have a distraction and hoping to learn more about this power she possessed. Meanwhile Mae went back to her normal life, avoiding the village as much as she could, she spent mornings at Bitter Brew. Conrad kept her mind off the door with new recipes and tasks around the café that Mae was reluctant to do but helped out anyway. With the warmer weather coming in Mae spent the hours before the sun came up on the cliff in the east, hoping Dori would return to their spot.

One day, Dori and several other students were pulled out of their honors Sun fairies class. In the gymnasium Dori automatically noticed her father along with the other council members sitting at a table in the middle of the gym. The towering glass ceiling was a perfect space for flying class, but now it supplied an ominous light over the table in the center with the council members sitting quietly watching the students enter. Many of her fellow students were already in the bleachers, as she took her seat with her classmates she looked to the left and there was Abigor standing in attention with a troop of other warriors.

Kenina sat in front of her looking over her shoulder, "Are you lost?" she sneered.

Dori looked ahead completely ignoring her, agitating Kenina. It was easy, Dori had become kind of numb to Kenina and most everything. Looking side to side there was an interesting collection of students in the bleachers, about a couple dozen, but Dori didn't notice any other Meta fairies. The bleachers were mostly filled with shades of white and orange as mostly Tempes and Sun fairies were in attendance, with a speckling of blue from the few water fairies mixed in among them.

Each council member was present, sitting at a long wooden table draped with the banners of the factions. The stones each of them held provided a gentle glow illuminating half the room. Each council elder was bestowed the stone of their magic; each time it was passed down the elder created a new holder for their stone for it to be with them at all times. Some wore it as a necklace or bracelet, others a staff they carried; Dori's favorite was Eirwen Kirsi, the Tempes fairy elder, whom wore her white stone in her crown of icicles. Dori adored how

Eirwen led with such poise and really connected to the people of the city. She was from up north from a long line of snow fairies. In attempts to bring more distant tribes of fairies into the city and have them accept the rule of the council, many decades ago they sought out leaders from those distant tribes and encouraged them to come to Zalor and take a role in the council. Eirwen jumped at the opportunity to make a difference for her people in Vilaríki and be a voice in the realm, Dori admired her courage.

The Sun Elder, Elio Solana, stood up and walked around the table. He was wearing what appeared to be battle gear, as her father's boss, Dori knew well enough that he didn't normally dress like that. His golden chest plate glistened in the light peaking through the cloudy skies above. The Sun gem was at the core of his chest, radiating a brilliant orange hue, casting a warm glow on the outline of the sun that was embossed on Elio's armor.

"Thank you all for disrupting your class schedules to meet with us today," Elios said pointing to the council members behind him. "With support from our guests from Nyaloa and Sororia, the council has devised a plan that requires your assistance."

The bleachers began to rumble with whispers.

"I understand there will be many questions but I ask you all to remain quiet until the end," Elio said sternly. Despite what he said it was obvious he was not asking. He gave the students a moment to quiet down. "The plan is simple, but requires a lot of power. We must come together and work as a people to defeat our enemies. As young fairies who have yet to declare their factions, your untapped powers hold special ability and we will need your strength."

Dori did not like where this was going.

"As we all know vampires cannot be in direct sunlight," Asteria said stepping up next to Elio. "Therefore the sun can be our greatest weapon."

"I have selected a collection of the strongest students to help aid in our mission," Elio continued. "Participation in this mission is entirely voluntary, and no one will face judgment for choosing to abstain. However, those who stand with us in our quest shall weave themselves into one of the most pinnacle moments in our history."

"We need as much fairy power as possible to preform our task," Asteria said. "Elios and Cyrus will lead the Sun fairies, and Isleen and Thaller will lead the Water and Tempes fairies from up on the side of Mount Seraphina." The Water fairy elder, Isleen, and her adjudicate Thaller nodded their heads in agreement. Eirwen's poise was unchanged, and her face hid her contempt well, but Dori could feel her negative energy from across the room, she did not approve of the actions being taken. Dori locked eyes with her father, he knew she shouldn't be here, her strength was in Meta but she was top of the Sun fairy class as well so of course she would be selected.

Isleen whisked her sea-blue hair out of her face and stood slowly. Asteria welcomed her up, giving her the floor. She walked with a gentle grace as her elaborate teal dress draped around her. "It has been centuries since any Water fairies were involved in any war on land, but our role is imperative," Isleen began. "We will go into greater detail and answer questions at another time, when we meet with those who decide to participate. We will work with Tempes to prepare the skies and be charged with containment," Isleen took a long pause glancing to the right at Elios, "So the Sun fairies may bring the sun to the wasteland of Cano Valley."

There was a collective gasp in the crowd, but no one dared speak as Elios and Asteria kept their eyes locked on the student body. They were the most intimidating members of the council, at least in Dori's opinion. They stood battle ready in the gym while Isleen stood with such poise she knew half the girls in her class were jealous of her siren-like beauty. Meanwhile old Foster Helm, the Dryad Elder, looked like he was about to fall asleep where he sat.

"Just as Meta fairies gather to form our borders, the Sun fairies who join us will gather together to direct the sun's rays on the valley, extinguishing every vampire possible," Elios said eyeing the students.

Dori swallowed hard doing her best not to react.

"The Night fairies will provide protection for the Sun fairies and make sure the effect is thorough," Asteria said.

Raging inside, Dori wanted to let her screams out. Those were people, they couldn't really plan to kill the entire village.

"As for the witches. Those who do not surrender and agree to leave the island will be executed," Asteria continued. "We will take back the east of the island, and after all is finished we will ignite the crest of Lithos Ridge again with the stones we hold, returning balance to our land," she said pointing to the council. Dori wanted to be sick.

As if on cue each council member that was still seated rose, Foster a bit delayed, and held their stone high. Foster with his wooden staff, Eirwen picking the crown off her head, Isleen lifting her wrist with the adorning bracelet up high. All gems ascended toward the light shining in through the glass glowing in a circle feet above them in the gymnasium, then slowly returned to their rightful elder.

"Not a word of this to anyone outside this room, we do not wish to worry our civilians," Asteria said. "The Spring Equinox is tomorrow, take the weekend, celebrate. Monday meet at the tower if you wish to participate. More details will come at that time," she tilted her head and turned back toward the Night fairies.

Looking at Abigor waiting for him to notice her, Dori was frantic. This couldn't happen, but she was just one teenager, how could she convince anyone this was wrong? If she knew one thing, it was once the council made up their mind there was no changing it. Her father sat there, looking at her for a while then was whisked away by Elio with orders.

Chatter began in the bleachers and they were dismissed back to their classes. It took everything in Dori not to scream at Kenina when she expressed how excited she was to be rid of the village. She simply stared at her walking through the hall and immediately went to Professor Lenora's study.

She barged in the door checking all around for any other soul in the room. "I'm not supposed to tell anyone but I need your advice, or maybe help. I don't know, all I know is I might explode and I can't go back to class," Dori rambled.

Lenora pulled her head back in surprise, eyes wide for a moment absorbing Dori's frantic rambling. Taking a breath she waved her hand over the door creating the barrier spell they used each day of their lessons when meeting here, and simply said, "I already know." Dori turned and looked at Lenora in question. "They came to me, all my years of experience they wanted to know if it would work," she said.

"And it will?" Dori asked, terrified of the answer.

"Yes, but I didn't tell them that. I told them they were wrong to take such action, and if they were unsuccessful it would be detrimental to our community," Lenora said. She looked at Dori and knew she was relieved. "And now they want you to partake," she said without question.

"Yeah! They've got fairies from all over convinced this is a good idea! It's ridiculous!" Dori bursted out, throwing her hands in the air.

"You need to help them," Lenora said calmly.

Dori stared at her like she was insane. "What?"

Lenora approached Dori resting her hands on her shoulders. "You are the most powerful fairy of this age, they need you," before Lenora finished Dori knew she wasn't talking about the fairies.

"*Mae* needs you."

CHAPTER 22

Lenora had a plan, but Dori would have to do it on her own. She arrived at the castle on Monday with several other students. She saw Sprig sitting on the fountain wall at the base of the tower.

"Hey Dori, this is the last place I thought I'd see you," Sprig said. "I didn't think Meta fairies were involved with this."

"You forget I'm still a Sun fairy, graduation isn't for a few months, I still have time before joining my faction," Dori said with a sarcastic smile.

"Still not sold on the whole factions thing huh?"

Dori simply shook her head taking a seat next to Sprig, not wanting to get into it in public.

"That's why I like you, not willing to be defined by one thing," Sprig said.

"Decided to come and help the cause," Dori said, not hiding her disdain for the idea.

Sprig smiled, "I'm assuming I'm here for the same reason you are," he said leaning in. "Need more information," he whispered and winked at her.

Dori looked at him, tilting her head in wonder, but as she opened her mouth to ask more Asteria walked in to guide the volunteers in their next steps.

Dividing into their factions they went to different sections of the city, Tempes fairies to the mountain peaks, Sun to the empty north beaches, Water to the Azure beach in the south, and the warriors divided to join the groups. Dori flew among a sea of orange, taking in the faces from all over Zalor and Meltembra; fairies of all ages, very few as young as herself and the small collection of students from Zalor High. They spent the day practicing channeling, gathering in groups to ignite small fires just from pulling rays from the sunlight. Heating up some sections of sand enough to make glass.

Sun augmentation, was not a power often utilized, even some of the older fairies hadn't had much practice in channeling; Dori was strong in her Sun magic but mainly because of her ability to control flame. Channeling on the other hand she was well-versed in as it was a prime practice for Meta fairies. Meta would often channel together to create a greater connection to the Einwhai, but Sun fairies didn't have many tasks that required a multitude of them to achieve. The group of Sun fairies worked on pulling the sun beams into the empty beach, brightening the north beach even as the sun was setting. Dori tried to hide the judgement on her face as she watched a group of fairies three times her age igniting the blue palm trees with the sun's rays and laughing about this new honed power. Watching the large blue leaves fall to the sand and turn to ash, she fought the urge to put the flames out.

They trained for hours, skipping dinner, which Dori was not used to, but she was determined to stick it out. A small handful of fairies left feeling they were not strong enough to endure the pressure, and Dori was determined not to be one of them, even if her stomach was growling.

They continued the same things for days, luckily providing food on the following days. Thursday they cut training short in the early afternoon and requested fairies go home to rest, they would be called any day to complete their mission, Dori had hoped they would lay out the specifics. She went straight home hoping her father would have more information.

Walking in the door to another Jareth episode, Dori rolled her eyes as she closed the door behind her.

"I heard about the plan at work, why didn't you ask me to join? You know I can't wait to be rid of those abominations," Jareth yelled at Cryus.

"You haven't even finished school Jareth," Cyrus said.

"I heard they were asking seniors!" He said just Dori walked in the room, "Is she a part of it?" Jareth yelled pointing at his sister.

"Jareth, you failed out of high school and were deterred from selecting your factions, they were very select with who they chose to be a part of this," Cryus responded growing in impatience.

"That wasn't a no!"

"This isn't a game or some competition you have with your sister, Jareth! This is war! And I've heard enough!" Cyrus yelled.

Jareth let out a scream and stomped off like a toddler, giving Dori a dirty look as he walked past her.

Dori barely looked at him and kept her eyes focused on her father standing in the living room face bright red. Now was not the time to push him, but she needed to know.

"Dad?"

"Not now Dori," Cyrus said turning his back on her.

She followed him into the kitchen and grabbed him some water as he plopped on one of the dining room chairs. "Dad, do they have a timeline of when this is going down?" she asked at a low volume as to not be overheard.

Cyrus looked up at her, grabbing the water, "Why did you volunteer?"

"I want to help," Dori said taking a seat.

"I know you better than that. You've never approved of the council making decisions without the vote of the people, especially something like this," Cyrus looked down.

"If you don't approve of this why are you going along with it?" Dori asked sincerely, feeling like she was about to have one of those bonding moments with her dad she strived for.

Cyrus looked at her but their moment was cut short by a knock at the door. Dori let out a sigh, and got up to answer the door. Cyrus grabbed her hand as she turned to walk away. Looking at her, his golden eyes flickering with the temptation of tears, he simply said "I believe in you, whatever you have to do."

He gave her hand a gentle squeeze and let her go. She almost forgot about the door with the weight of his words holding a tight grip on her heart, then there was another knock.

To her surprise she opened the door to find Abigor.

"Hey," he said with a smile. "Can we grab a quick bite?"

After a quick change and saying hi to her mom, Dori and Abigor were off. Abigor asked about school and her friends during dinner, keeping the conversation focused on her mostly, which was new. After dinner they took a walk, enjoying the night falling on the city and the glowing auroras appearing above the castle.

As Dori was admiring the purple and green lights swinging across the sky Abigor grabbed her hands.

"Endora," he began.

Dori's eyes widened.

"Tomorrow is a big day, and I'm not sure what's going to happen," Abigor said, playing with her hands in his.

Tomorrow. Dori realized she got the answer she was seeking for earlier.

"You and the other student fairies will be summoned early. But the attack will happen at sunrise," Dori's mind was racing with this information and completely forgot about the young man before her holding her hands. "And with all that's at risk I just want you to know how much I care about you."

That slap in the face brought her back to reality.

"We've been through so much, and I truly care for you," Abigor said, raising his eyes from her hands to her face. "Please be cautious, the mountains won't be in direct fire but you are still in a war-zone and if anything goes wrong, promise me you will get out. I know you are a powerful Sun fairy, but I want you to be safe," Abigor said, reaching for the sun necklace he gave her. Dori hadn't worn it in months but knew he would notice at dinner if she wasn't wearing it.

"I'm not a Sun fairy," the words just slipped out. Of all the things jumbling in her mind that was the one that came out.

"Not yet, why do you think I got you the sun necklace? You're obviously going to be a Sun fairy. I've heard great things about you in practice too, you're going to impress a lot of important people tomorrow," Abigor said with a hue of arrogance.

"Abigor—" Dori wanted to ask about how he *cares* for her but he stopped her from talking.

"I know you're strong, but promise me you'll stay on the mountain. You'll be miles away from the fire, literally. Stay on the mountain and I will see you when it's over," Abigor smiled then leaned in and kissed her on the lips.

The most passion he had shown her in months, a loving lip-lock that should have felt like something to her, but it didn't.

"Go get some rest, I'll see you tomorrow, when it's a new world," Abigor said and fluttered off without another word.

Dori watched the fairy fly away from her, frozen in place with so much more to say. A bright purple jolt reflected in the water by her feet, she looked back up at the auroras and she was suddenly brought back to reality.

Mae.

She whipped out her phone.

SOS. Meet at our spot. NOW!

Dori sent the text then looked around to see if anyone could see her. Flittering into fairy form Dori created a bubble around herself to remain unseen. She made it to the edge of the barrier in the east and flew straight through, she kept a trained eye on all her surroundings and stayed in her little invisible bubble until she saw Mae appear near the cliff where they first met.

Dori landed next to Mae, dispersing the bubble around her. Mae gasped, stepping back knocking some pebbles right off the edge of the cliff to the ocean below, but was still bitter enough to ignore her surprise. "Look who finally decided to show up," she said with a huff as she crossed her arms in front of her.

Jutting her head forward, Dori blinked aggressively looking at Mae. "Show up?" She flung her arm behind her pointing at the mountains. "I've been locked in Meltembra for *months*," she seethed, anger taking over her at Mae's absurd comment.

"You could've called, texted! Something!"

"Back at yah!" Dori snapped.

"You're the one that walked away!" Mae began to yell.

"Ahhh!" Dori threw her hands up. "We don't have time for this! The fairies are coming!"

"What are you talking about?"

"The fairies, a lot of them, they are going to attack, at sunrise," Dori said with sadness staining her aggression.

Mae stepped back shaking her head. "They're coming here?" She asked pointing behind her in the direction of the village. "What do they plan on doing?"

Dori stared at her ashamed to answer.

"Dori," Mae said sternly taking a step back towards her friend. "What are they planning?"

"They're going to clear the skies," Dori said raising a hand to her face, pressing her fingers into her temple. "They're going to bring the sun rays down on the village," her voice now devoid of anger.

"They can do that?"

Dori just gave a nod, both hands pressed on her temples, eyes now strained on the ground.

"What about the witches? They don't burn in the sun."

"They will be given a chance to surrender, or..." Dori couldn't even finish the sentence, picking her face up to look at Mae. "It's barbaric! And I can't believe they would do it, but they are so set on vengeance and making sure nothing like the bombing ever happens again."

Looking at her friend with pleading eyes, suddenly a couple of vampires showed up next to Mae and before Dori could react she felt a tight squeeze on the back of her neck. Pain and fear surged through her as her feet lifted into the air, dangling over the crashing ocean below.

CHAPTER 23

Ignoring the long cold fingers squeezing the back of her neck she strained her eyes to the side to look at the vampire holding her up in the air as she heard Mae yell "Zagan, let go of her."

Her eyes pained her as she tried to get a good look at the old vampire she had heard so much about. "So you're the *tick* that ruined my best friend's life," Dori said, barely able to look at the figure that held her dangling in the air.

Zagan tightened his grip on her neck, his long discolored fingernails breaking into her skin and drawing blood. Breathing in the scent of her blood, Zagan pulled Dori closer to him as his canine teeth grew longer. Dori finally got a good look at the old vampire as he twisted his head around the side of her. She looked at his large black eyes, half covered by his grotesque protruding forehead with his slightly greyed skin and layers of wrinkles. Dori had heard about vampires like this, the more human life they took the more demonic they look. He must've taken a lot of life to be *that* ugly, Dori thought.

"Don't you dare!" Mae screamed, trying to pull away from the two vampires holding her back.

"Silence," Dori heard a woman say from behind Mae, then she saw a hand reach up and with a flick of her wrist, still feet away from Mae, the woman snapped her neck.

"Mae!"

The stunning woman walked into view completely ignoring Dori's cries. Her dark face was painted with drippings of gold running down her cheeks, golden flames framing her eyes, and a crescent moon painted in the middle of her forehead. Her eyes were a bright sapphire blue as if they were glittering gems. There was no doubt she was one of the Seraphina.

"Zagan, may I remind you what fairy blood does to you?"

Zagan closed his mouth and threw Dori down to the side, staring at the witch.

"Did she reveal their plan?" She asked.

"Yes, Avyanna. They will be attacking at dawn," Zagan said.

Avyanna nodded then leaned down toward Dori. Dori was mesmerized by her bright eyes as her long black eyelashes bat around them. Before she could even react to Avyanna approaching, the witch clasped heavy bangles around her wrists. Dori's breath was stolen as her power was immediately diminished.

Avyanna gave a coy smile, "That ought to hold her for a while," she said standing back up. "Put them both in the dungeon in the mansion," she said to the brutes holding the lifeless Mae.

One of them got wide eyes and looked at the other, "The creepy dungeon," he whispered.

Zagan hissed at them and in a flash, one threw Mae over his shoulder and the other picked Dori up off the ground and they sped off down the hill toward the village.

Mae awoke in a dingy old cell next to Dori, who was sitting on the ground chained to the brick wall. She lifted her head dazed, staring around the dirty floor and rusted bars.

"Dori? Where are we?" Mae asked confused.

Dori rolled her head over to stare at Mae, "They said the mansion," she muttered.

Mae chuckled. "Finally made it to the mansion, I thought the inside would be nicer," she said smiling at Dori. Now that she was more alive, literally, she realized the state of her friend. Rushing over to her side she pulled at the chains around her wrists.

"It's some kind of magic blocker," Dori said as Mae broke the chain free from the wall.

Mae attempted to pull the thick bangles from her wrists but it burned at the touch.

"Mae, I'm sorry," Dori said hoarsely.

"You don't have to be sorry, I got you into this mess. I should've known they would be watching me after the necklace issue," Mae said, saddened. "You were right to stay away."

Trying to catch her breath, gasping for air, Dori reached out and grabbed Mae's hand.

"What is happening to you?"

"A fairy without magic...is nothing," Dori said plainly. "There is no life apart from it." Then she winced in pain and her shackles clashed on the ground as she reached for her side. The air caught in her throat as it always did when the pain flared.

Mae tried not to sound frantic, "What? What's happening?"

Dori could barely get the words out as the escalating pain choked the air from her, "My healing magic—" she clenched her eyes shut and grimaced at the pain.

"Shit," Mae cursed, in a concerned voice. "Let me see your side."

Dori shook her head and mouthed no, but no sound escaped her throat.

"Endora, show me your side," Mae demanded aggressively, as she reached for Dori's shirt. As she pulled it back and gave a small gasp her friend looked up at her with red eyes. "Dori, why is your skin grey?"

Dori was confused, to her it always appeared blueish, like bruising, she had no idea what Mae was talking about.

"Okay," Mae shook her fear from her mind and redirected herself. "How do we get these off? It's witch magic right, you're supposed to be able to counter it?" Mae said frantically. "What about your dimensional magic!

If you had a covering, like you did for me with the necklace, it would protect you from the chains right?"

"Theoretically," Dori muttered. "But there's nothing down here to channel, no sun, and no—" she broke off, intense thought in her eyes.

"No what?"

Dori smiled at her, "You," she paused, "Meta fairies thrive from positive emotion, you are the answer." Already the idea was livening her spirit.

"What?" Mae looked at her like she was crazy.

"My best friend, you bring the most light in my life, I just need to channel enough to surround my wrists and I can break the connection," she said holding her wrists up in pain.

Mae grabbed Dori before she slumped over in the dirt. "What do you need me to do?"

"Tell me something. Anything. About our friendship," Dori said looking up at her.

"Uhhh, okay," Mae thought for a moment, "Remember when we ate our weight in funnel cake at the Harvest Festival, and you sneezed and sent powdered sugar flying everywhere?" Mae laughed remembering the moment, she sat there for several minutes listing off conversations and inside jokes. Making Dori smile, but she was still fading, her face looking almost grey in the gloomy cell.

"Like I said, it was just a theory," Dori said choking. "I'm not strong enough."

"Bull," Mae said, sitting her up straighter. "The girl who *'accidentally'* spilled a slushy on a guy who made fun of me at the mall is strong, fierce, and amazing. The girl who sticks up to her abusive brother even when it means coming to me with singed hair and tears in her eyes." Mae grabbed ahold of Dori's arms and looked her straight in the eyes. "She is the most powerful girl I've ever met."

Dori almost cried then and there. Without thinking her hands glowed yellow and the chains broke and turned to dust the instant they hit the ground.

The friends embraced each other and held on for dear life as Dori's color returned to her face.

"Can you get us out of here? I need to get to Lithos Ridge," Dori looked at Mae.

"I'm still weak from whatever they gave me, probably a shot of cinnamon oil," Mae said, giving the cell bars a shake. "I don't have the strength."

Dori took Mae's hand, channeling the power within Mae. Mae's body gave one violent shake and she felt renewed. Dori smirked at her and nodded.

Mae didn't even question Dori's plan, she trusted her completely. Getting up she turned and in one movement charged the bars of the cell, bursting them off the ground. She turned back to her friend mouth wide open in amazement. The two brutes who brought them there heard the commotion and the wooden door 30 feet away flew open. Mae met them in an instant, bolting in a second across the rusted corridor, sticking her hands right in their chests and removing their hearts.

Dori had never seen Mae be so violent, she could feel her heart threatening to beat through her chest. A sense of fear stole her nerves, but she had never experienced someone going to such great lengths to protect her, which made her feel empowered and uplifted, and she needed to focus on that feeling if she was going to face what awaited her outside this dungeon. She swallowed her fears and grabbed handfuls of the dust from the chains and stuck it in her pockets. The friends walked out of the dungeon and as Mae snapped a few vampires necks, Dori spotted a blood bag one of them had obviously intended for themselves. Tossing it to Mae to build up her strength Dori flicked her wrists tossing back anyone else that approached the duo. A dozen vampires later the two walked out the towering double doors and sauntered down the large staircase away from the mansion.

Flitting into fairy form Dori turned to Mae and waved her hand to swirl around her, "Hold on." Mae stared at the tiny version of her friend as she was covered in a dance of yellow and orange sparkles. Mae was astonished when Dori, the size of a doll, lifted her into the air with ease.

In an instant, they soared through the skies above Cano Valley, invisible to the world below. As the sun peeked above the horizon, Mae's gaze fixated on its celestial dance with a mix of alarm and wonder, a sight long unseen. The radiant sun painted the waves below in hues of orange and red, a breathtaking spectacle that overshadowed any fear of plummeting during the flight.

Landing just at the base of the cliff, Dori paused, turning back to human size. Judging by the lack of vampires alerted to their presence Mae assumed they were still in Dori's barrier. She stared at Dori wondering why they stood at the base of the hill.

"I've never seen this side of Lithos Ridge," Dori said, slowly approaching the statue of Kairos. Looking his gargoyle face straight in the eye she said, "Now that I'm here, all I feel is darkness."

Mae looked past her friend at the rising sun, "Dori, I have to get inside," she said, placing a hand on her arm.

Turning to face her friend, "I can help with that." She put her hands on either side of Mae, grabbing her arms tenderly. With eyes closed she broke the barrier around them, which Mae was able to see as a bubble of yellow burst around them and sparkles rushed towards Dori. The waves and wisps of sparkling yellow and purple hung in the air around Dori then rushed down her arms and Mae felt a surge of energy as the light traveled from Dori's arms to her own.

"What did you just do?"

"It's like your necklace, but it's temporary," she said and began to squeeze harder. "You feel heat you find shelter. It should last a couple hours at least but if anything happens to me it could falter."

"What do you mean if something happens to you," Mae asked anxiously.

"Mae, I know what I need to do, but it's going to take a lot of power," Dori said turning back to look at the ridge beyond the statue. She stood watching the sun, "Can you keep them away from the ridge?" She asked before turning to face Mae.

"Whatever you need," Mae said reaching out and grabbing Dori's hands. "I won't let them near you." Mae looked deep into Dori's eyes, the sister she had always dreamed of, she wouldn't dare let anything happen to her.

Dori smiled and released her friend's hands. She turned to walk up the slope, taking a deep breathe walking past Kairos staring him down.

"Dori," Mae called out.

Dori turned to face her.

"Remember how powerful you are," Mae said with a gently serious look.

Dori's mouth curved ever so slightly in a somber smile and gave a nod. Turning back around she stared at the lifeless stone hedges standing in a u-shape mere feet from the edge of the tall cliff. The further she walked the feeling of darkness grew stronger around her. But if she was successful, she could change that.

"I am strong," she said to herself. "I am powerful. I am enough," she spoke into the distance as a tear crept into her eye. She stood with her toes at the edge of stone circle at the entrance to the ridge. Taking a step forward, the ridge pulled her down and she collapsed to her knees.

CHAPTER 24

Mae heard Dori hit the ground and ran to help her. Hearing Mae cry out for her, Dori put a hand up behind her creating a wall barrier just behind the statue to block entrance to the ridge. Mae slammed her fists on the barrier. Dori stood slowly and turned to face Mae and the valley. Her eyes were glowing red.

"I'm fine," she said at a low volume, knowing Mae would still hear her. "Go warn the villagers to stay indoors, the fairies will be here soon."

Mae's lip twitched angrily as she stared at her friend, reluctantly she forced herself to turn and do as Dori said.

Dori savored each slow breath, attuning her senses to the symphony of waves crashing against the cliff's foundation. Each surge sent shivers of vitality through her, as if the ocean itself caressed her skin with its watery embrace. The red faded from her eyes and she felt the pressure release. She trailed her hands in the air in front of each stone circling the ridge. Directly below her, in a way, was the stone hedges with the power gems. There were two of each stone, the council member of each faction held one and the stones in the ridge held the others. When the worlds were separated this copy of the ridge was created. Though it has never been proven, Lenora believed that the gems power could still be reached from this side. Which is why the Seraphina had come here all those years ago and possibly aided in how the vampire race was created.

Staring at the empty space in the middle of the 7 stones, Dori pictured the Queen's statue that stood in her realm. Pulling her hands up, waving her fingers as if commanding a gentle ensemble. She turned to each stone surrounding her and pictured its twin in the realm below, each full of color and power, while she stared down the lifeless grey replica. Each stone still had etchings like each of the others, the Dryad stone with leaves and vines, the Night stone with its stars and echos of distance planets; it was as if it signified the death of magic. Finally she came to the stone that sat at the head of the cliff, the Meta stone looked more lifeless than the rest. Without the bright glimmering wisps the etchings looked so empty and bleak.

Just like life without magic. Dori thought.

Head titled down, hands at her sides with palms facing the stone, she raised her eyes angrily staring at the empty space where the Meta power gem would sit. Her arms slowly rose and she pulled with all her might into herself, summoning the magic below.

Lenora taught Dori much about Alchemy magic, but any time she brought up King and Queen Amara, Lenora would change the subject, always saying she would share more when Dori was ready. And despite her hopes, her Council History never touched on the birth of the council, only how it has been run and council members selected over the last millennia. She knew there was more to the story, hidden from all the history books, and standing here now gave her a feeling of wonder. After all this maybe Lenora would finally share the information she held back.

A commotion began in the village below quickly growing louder, Dori turned and saw the reason why. She saw the army of fairies on the side of the mountain beyond the volcano. The wave of small figures in flight separated; a stream of blue and white sparkle showed the Water and Tempes fairies flying up higher on the mountain, a surge of orange glistened along the side of the volcano as the Sun fairies took their post, and a glittering black swarm rolled its way toward the village. Dori saw Mae return to the base of the cliff. They exchanged looks then Dori shut her eyes.

Standing at the center ring in the middle of stones Dori reached her hands out to the side and stood still. Without realizing it she began to float, when she opened her eyes she was 5 feet in the air now eye level with the group of fairies on the side of the volcano. In the corners of her eyes she could see her wings, glowing brighter than ever before, shades of purple, pink hues from the orange, light from the yellow, even shades of deep blue purple as she channeled the power of the waves. Her heart beat steady.

Mae stood, mouth gaped open as she watched her friend effortlessly floating mid-air in full fairy form while remaining her natural size. She smiled with pride.

Feeling the power surge within her Dori's eyes were shut as she let the sensation flow through her, radiance cascading down her extremities. She opened her eyes suddenly when she heard a voice call to her.

"Endora, my child," the voice said.

Twisting back toward the ocean, looking past her shining wing, Dori saw a figure in the sky, as if it was breaking through from the fae realm, surrounded by glistening light. Her hair shone bright red leading into purple tips very much like her own, while her piercing green eyes stared into her soul.

"Do not believe the lies they sell you," said the woman in the sky.

"Who are you?"

The woman smiled. "You have done well. You mustn't fear the darkness, nor be ashamed of it," she said elegantly. "Know all you endure will make you more powerful." The words sat like silk on her skin.

Just before the woman disappeared Dori noticed a black crown adorned on her head. "Dahlia?"

The ashy clouds over her head began to move toward the ocean, Dori turned to see fairies scattered amongst the shelf of ash. Tempes fairies cleared the clouds spinning in tiny tornados wafting the air around them, clearing spots within the ash so the Sun fairies could drag the rays through to the valley. The sun was now fully visible over the horizon and the light began to shine on the land. Mae had done a proficient job in getting most vampires inside but some stood in the shadows of the buildings waiting to protect their home. Many of the Seraphina stood in the center of the valley chanting. The clouds continued to clear and the village was seeing sunlight for the first time in its existence.

As light illuminated the side of the volcano, Night fairies began coming around, descending into the village, allowing the sun to lead their steps. Warriors armed with stakes and daggers looked more like mercenaries than the protectors they were meant to be. Dori clasped her hands together then spread her arms across the skies, creating a thick barrier in the sky above, between the clouds and the village below, the same barrier she had given Mae. The sunlight shown below but the rays did not penetrate. The vampires hesitated looking at the shimmering sky above, but with Night fairies fast approaching the village they sped forward flashing their teeth, eager for blood. Night fairies fought off vampires that approached the Sun fairies as the rays of light crested over the buildings coming toward the side of the volcano. Light hit the vampires and they quivered waiting for the heat but it didn't come. The devilish smiles spread across them as they readied themselves to return to the fight. Wooden stakes were flying around turning vampires to dust, and fairies were being ripped apart in a flash, left lifeless in pools of blood on the side of the volcano.

Abruptly, a loud crack shook the earth below their feet and the fighting stopped as fairies and vampires tried to stand steady. The Tempes fairies continued to clear the skies untouched by the quake, Sun fairies gathered themselves quickly in attempts to break the barrier.

Dori's voice rang out above the clammer, "ENOUGH!"

Fairies, vampires, and witches looked in amazement having not noticed the shimmering beauty floating above Lithos Ridge.

"This battle is not ours! We have taken on the war of our ancestors and we cannot continue it. Witch magic and fairy magic do not have to be enemies!" Dori said her voice carrying throughout the hills.

"Kill her," the brutal order echoed from the cowardly leader of the vampires who had finally decided to join the party. A dozen vampires sped off without hesitation.

Elio Solana barked at the Sun fairies, "Why have you stopped? Pull the sunlight through!"

Asteria followed suit and reminded her Night fairies of their orders, "To the village. They will surrender or die. Drag the vampires out of their homes if need be."

Dori saw the fighting resume and bit her lip in frustration. She took a deep breath and illuminated the barrier again making sure it remained strong as Mae stood at the base of the ridge breaking the necks of any vampires who approached, not wanting to kill those who were simply protecting their loved ones. As Night fairies marched through the village, Dori did all she could to use her magic and flicked them left and right keeping them away from the valley dwellers, but the barrier was already weakening her.

Beams of light began to break through the barrier, and Tempes fairies shot through it blasting holes in the buildings, tearing some roofs completely off. Dori strained in the sky and watched a vampire go up in flames next to Mae as she stood safe in the sunlight with Dori's protection spell still on her skin. When another vampire began to catch fire a rush of water came billowing through the air and put out the flames. Dori looked to the left and as the water dispersed she saw Sprig, standing on the outskirts of the village arms still reached out as the water returned to his side. Mae gave him a nod of gratitude. Dori was relieved to have another powerful fairy on her side, a feeling that helped aid her strength again.

Dori landed next to him, "What took you so long?" She asked smiling.

Sprig looked at her with a chuckle, pulling circling balls of water up in his hands. "Duck," he said raising his eyebrows, shooting a ball of water in her direction. Dori dropped to the ground and the water ball took out a vampire coming up behind her. "I would say you look awful, but you look stunning," he added admiring her wings as she stood again. "What do you need?"

She smiled, "A hand," she uttered reaching out her hand. Sprig didn't hesitate and grabbed her forearm and looked her deep in the eyes, giving her a jolt of his magic. Dori gave a nod trying not to think about the tingles traveling up her arm.

Sprig pulled her closer, "You got this," he whispered releasing her arm and she shot back into the sky.

Dori thrust her hands into the sky as she ascended, yellow sparkles shot out in every direction reinforcing the barrier. A tiny scream caught her attention and she saw Abigor removing a stake from his holster, approaching a young vampire holding a child in her arms. Before he even had a chance to raise his arm Dori dropped from the sky in front him.

"No," Dori said standing tall in his way, "They have no fight with us."

Abigor stood amazed, mesmerized by the glistening purple wings emanating from Dori's back.

"Fight with us, or I will put you down," Dori threatened before taking flight back to the ridge.

Speechless, Abigor reached his hand up as she flew away.

Returning to the ridge, Dori called out to Sprig. She pointed her face to the sky and threw the dust from her pocket in the air. Sprig lifted his hands and coated the base of the barrier in a cloud of sparkling dust.

Dori swirled her arms, followed by her entire body. She flew forward blasting the sparkling mist to the side of the volcano. A cracking noise pierced her ears and she turned toward the statue at the base of Lithos Ridge. A crack traveled up the side of the King's body, then stopped after splitting the outer layer of the statue. She looked at it in confusion but shook her head and continued swirling the mist.

Dori hovered over the buildings of the village as she heard Sprig cry out behind her. Turning to witness a vampire with his hand in Sprig's chest, her mouth barely fell open before his heart was ripped from his chest. Pain struck her as her lip quivered and tears welled in her eyes. Mae rushed to Sprig throwing a stake she stole from a Night fairy seconds earlier straight at the vampire turning him to dust, leaving the remaining skeleton to drop to the ground. She caught the young fairy before he hit the ground. His bright blue eyes faded to black and Mae closed his lids as his body turned limp. She looked up at Dori to reassure her, Dori let out a stuttering breath turning back to the clouds, attempting to push through her pain.

"Swallow your pain," she uttered to herself doing all she could to stay afloat in the sky. She beat the pain growing in her side with her fist, grit her teeth and uttered it again, something she was used to doing. "Swallow the pain," the words bled from her tongue. But she couldn't hold it in and let out a scream throwing her head back and arms out as light came bursting out of her chest and the dust from the anti-magic shackles shot out in every direction.

All at once the mist fell upon the village below her, sadly it didn't have quite the affect that Dori was hoping for but witches, fairies, and vampires grew weak and the fighting slowed. Now floating at the center above them all, Dori observed them all descend near the ground, weary but all eyes trained on her.

"Please," Dori pleaded. "Why continue on the hatred that was passed along. Can we not choose for ourselves the beliefs we have about one another?"

Dazed eyes of slowly moving magical creatures looked at her and one another, then she heard a violent scream. Quickly turning to the source of the shriek, she saw Zagan with his teeth sunken into Avyanna's neck. Dori was so taken aback by Zagan attacking his strongest witch she couldn't have possibly anticipated his next move. Channeling the witch's blood now flowing through his veins, he leapt from the ground launching himself off the side of a building straight at her. Dori placed a hand in front of her as a reflex and somehow caught Zagan midair and he stayed there frozen. His eyes bolted back and forth the only part of him that was able to move.

Out of nowhere, Mae jumped from below grabbing Zagan's ankle and pulling him to the ground with a hard smack. In one swift movement she leapt on top of him and drove a wooden stake in his chest. The sound of his breastplate cracking rung in her ears as Zagan gasped.

"I warned you not to touch her," Mae snarled in his greying face before his flesh burst into dust leaving nothing but a grotesque skeleton behind. Gasps came from every direction.

Dori rushed to Avyanna, placing a hand on her gaping neck. The blood gurgled in her throat as she gasped for air. Dori's hand surged with yellow light, "Please, help me end this," she asked through teary eyes.

Avyanna sat up feeling her neck, "After what we did?" Dori simply stared into her eyes, telling her all she needed to. Avyanna rose, "Asteria!" Dori watched as the Night fairy appeared from the crowd, limping as blood trailed down her leg. "The girl is right, my ancestors brought Zagan here, and I do not wish to carry on that legacy."

Dori stood up as Elio descended from the sky above spinning into human form landing in front of Avyanna. His shoulders broad and face stern. "And we are supposed to trust in what exactly? A truce?"

"Under Zagan's rule we have lived as slaves to his cruelty. I have known nothing else in my life," Avyanna said. "I beseech you, give us the chance to recover from the mistakes of the generations before us," Avyanna looked at Dori with regret. "And the mistakes we ourselves have made."

Asteria stayed quiet eyeing the witch. Dori looked around as strength seemed to be returning back to the creatures before her, in moments everything could turn back to bloodshed. Dori opened her mouth to speak but didn't know what she could possibly say to sway Asteria to peace.

Suddenly a small orange light came down and Cyrus popped out of it. "Asteria," he said boldly and out of breath. "We've lost enough today." Dori felt a pang in her heart and looked back at the place where Sprig's body lay, trying to keep her composure.

"He's right," Elio added. "We cannot act in haste. Let the council convene." Elio turned to Avyanna. "If it is as you say, I expect a new leader will lead into a new age. Long ago our people once proposed a treaty."

"And this time we will accept it," Avyanna said without hesitation.

"And my people will make sure you *uphold* it," Asteria finally spoke, viciously.

Mae grabbed Dori's shoulder, turning her toward her and aggressively pulled her in for a hug, her wings finally disappearing back into her body. Dori released Mae from the hug and walked through the crowd of supernatural creatures still regaining their strength. She knelt down next to Sprig lifting his head onto her lap, gently moving a piece of blue hair away from his closed eyes. "I'm so sorry," she whimpered as tears strolled down her cheeks, she pulled Sprig's limp body in for one last hug.

Picking up her head, Dori watched the supernatural creatures of Delmira Island aiding those they once claimed as their enemies. Tempes fairies floating above the buildings returning the dark clouds and once again hiding the sun from the valley. Witches placing healing concoctions on injured fairies' limbs. From a few houses down she faintly heard Elio say "a new era" while shaking Avyanna's hand.

Placing Sprig back down and stood up again as Mae approached her.

"A new era indeed," Dori said attempting to focus on the hope of peace as she wrapped her arms around her best friend and let out a whimper.

Chapter 25

Abigor appeared next to them and Mae gave him a dirty look while stepping away to give them a minute.

"Hi," Dori said plainly, wiping a tear from her face.

"Dori," Abigor said grabbing her hands. "You were incredible. I've never seen anything like that," he said pulling her in for a hug.

Dori felt warmth spread over here in the affection she had longed for.

Releasing her from the hug, Abigor smiled at her. "You created all this," he said pointing to the creatures around them. "You created peace after generations of hate. You truly are powerful." He looked her in the eyes and said the three words that should have made her gleam. "I love you."

The words stung for a moment but Dori felt her power overtake her. "Yesterday you 'cared' for me," she said, cocking her head to the side. "But today, after I express my power, you love me."

Abigor responded surprised. "I've always loved you, from the moment we met, I've always seen how influential you are capable of being and pushed you to be strong and powerful. I know we have been going through a hard time, but I was wrong and just needed to be reminded of how amazing you are," he said reaching for her arm, "of how much I love you."

Dori gave a small smile. "Goodbye, Abigor," she said squeezing his hands. "I am worth more than the scraps you offer." She turned and walked away from him.

Mae's jaw dropped, having heard the whole thing she rushed to Dori in the crowd. Dori, startled by her friend's sudden appearance, was still shaking from the encounter. "I'm so proud of you," Mae said, hugging her best friend. And again Dori felt her anxieties leave, knowing she had done the right thing.

Dori was lucky to have her father's connections. Cyrus had her back and reminded the council that if not for her actions, which allowed the peace to be brokered, there would have been far more casualties. It helped that they were busy dealing with the repercussions of making war advancements without the knowledge or vote of the people of Zalor. Returning to school on Monday was a nightmare, most people would have loved the attention but Dori hated it, especially as Kenina kept spouting lies about how it all went down.

"Of course I helped the vampires, it was wrong of the council to order them executed," she would tell people. "I convinced sweet fragile Dori to use her Meta powers to create a barrier above the village."

The council published a story in the news about the young up-and-coming fairy that used her light powers to create the illusion of her large wings to help sway the cause; claiming it was part of the plan all along. That the fairies merely needed to show their power and pull the village away from Zagan's influence to broker a peace. The way so many other students talked about the encounter was wild, Dori couldn't believe some of the outlandish stories being told. She was happy when Lenora ordered a stop to the gossip the moment her class began. The only normal class she had attended all day.

After class was over, Dori sat in her seat waiting to speak with the professor alone. Immediately after the door shut behind the last student Lenora cast a barrier over it and stood quietly leaning against her desk.

"Dori," Lenora said gently, raising a hand to welcome her over.

Dori walked over and Lenora grabbed her hands holding them tightly.

With tears welling in her eyes Lenora looked at Dori, "You are so much more powerful than I could have ever imagined," she said. "And I am afraid I have put in you in grave danger."

Dori just stared at her professor.

"I told you to keep your Alchemy power a secret, and luckily from what I have heard no one is talking about that power. They merely believe it was the use of both your strengths of Meta and Sun," Lenora said, biting her lip. "I wonder what the council members must be thinking after witnessing your remarkable abilities and noticing that your wings are completely purple."

Dori gulped fear running through her at the mere sound in Lenora's voice.

"You must keep your head down, do not show anymore great power unless completely necessary. There is so much I want to tell you but now is not the time."

"Like about Dahlia?"

Lenora squeezed her hands a bit tighter. "I need you to trust me. With graduation around the corner, even though everyone will tell you to select your faction you need to defer," Lenora pleaded. "There is a school where you can go. You can continue to work on this magic in secret, say you would like more time to choose between Sun and Meta, nothing more. The council's cover-up story is working well, now what I need from you is to do your best to stay off their radar."

There was nothing more for Dori to say, she trusted Lenora even if she was hiding things. She nodded in compliance.

Lenora smiled at her and released her hands. "Go on, head off to your next class."

Turning back briefly on her way to the door, "She told me not to fear the darkness, that all of this would make me stronger," Dori said gently.

"Who told you?" Lenora asked, confused.

"Dahlia."

In the following months, the fairies helped rebuild all they had destroyed in Cano Valley, and the witches and vampires offered materials and food to the fairies as they continued to rebuild the east side of Zalor.

Lenora was right and focus quickly shifted off of her amazing winged spectacle to the upcoming Zalor High graduation. However, the short memories of the public only fueled Jareth's mockery.

"I can't believe people were saying you were human size with wings," Jareth laughed. "Some all powerful fairy, you can't even decide on a faction."

"Jareth, that's enough. Your sister can defer, she's going to go to school and decide later," Adelyn interjected. Dori smiled at her mother coming to her defense.

Jareth grunted before storming off. Dori knew it absolutely drove him nuts that she, his younger sister, was finishing high school before him. He had failed out the year before and the council refused to allow him a faction selection before he completed school. Ever since receiving her acceptance letter a couple weeks prior she just counted down the days til she would be leaving this house. Making the most of her time with Blythe and Mae before she moved away to school.

Llyrfen University was a long drive from the mainland ports near the island; heading north-west toward the Great Lakes, only a short drive from Niagara Falls. Dori couldn't wait to be somewhere where no one knew her, the campus was a beautiful secluded little school, at least in the human world. In Meltembra it was an elaborate ancient school where fae from all over came to study the complexities of magic. Lenora said she knew the headmistress many years ago and that Dori would be safer there learning more about Alchemy magic, rather than in Zalor where the council loomed over the city.

A lot had changed in the last months and Dori's life would continue to change as she moved away to college and finally got the fresh start she was ready for. The peace between the communities on the island had benefited everyone, even though some did not agree with the change in status quo. Asteria continued to fight the rest of the council on fighting the creatures of the dark, as it was their duty as Night fairies. Of course it would take time to open the minds of those stuck on traditional ways. Dori and Mae got to hang out in public, so it really benefited them. With Zagan gone Mae's community had begun to flourish, Dori even got to see her house and meet her family, her dad wasn't a fan but her mom and brothers welcomed her with open arms. The Seraphina witches were freer than they had been in over a century, and the very land around them began to benefit from their use of natural magic. They connected to their deep fairy roots they were unaware of and flourished. Avyanna had been so grateful to Dori for saving her, that she dedicated her time to gaining knowledge of witch and fairy history to right the direction of her people.

Walking in graduation without much care about the whole thing, Dori watched her friends and classmates choose their factions. Lily and Sage blessed with an ancient oak joining Dryad, Kenina showing off her golden sun pendant as she joined Sun, and her fellow Meta classmates adorned in beaming yellow sashes of light.

The Elder from the Meta faction, Dusan Alastor, walked up to Dori after the ceremony, sending a shiver down her spine. His bright-yellow-cat-like eyes were surprisingly the least terrifying thing about him, Asteria and Elio were nothing compared to Dusan and his dedication to the faction system. The whole Alastor line were devoted Meta fairies who stuck firmly to the traditions passed down to them. Towering over her, Dusan peered his yellow eyes into hers and looked deep into her soul. "Endora Teresi," he said with question lingering on his lips. "Knowing how strong you are I am quite surprised to see you as a deferal student," he said as if it were an insult. "I know your father was hoping you would join the Sun faction, but someone with your—*potential*—" he paused, letting the word sting the air around her, "Would be a great asset to the Meta faction."

Fighting the tightening of her throat Dori choked down a breath, "Well, I am powerful in both Sun and Meta," she paused, grasping courage to continue, "I just want to be sure I make the right choice," she said with the shame of the lie making her ears twitch. She was indeed powerful in both, but she would do anything not to be forced to choose, to be able to continue pursuing the melding of magics.

"Yes," he said with all the stench of judgement. "Shame really, I was looking forward to you interning at the tower this summer," he uttered, tilting his head like a Hydra Viper waiting to sink its teeth in. "And rather unfortunate to hear about you and young Abigor, the council was eager for a strong couple such as yourselves to help lead," he added with raised eyebrows of pure judgement. Dori swallowed hard, plenty of people had mentioned that to her in the past weeks, but it sat heavier on her coming directly from a council member. "Be it so, Meta looks forward to you being a bright part of our future." Dusan walked off head held high clutching his staff with the beaming Meta gem atop the intricate twining of gold, etched with ancient symbols.

Dori felt like she was being pulled in so many directions, but she wasn't done learning about Alchemy yet and knew she made the right decision. Still, she hated interactions like that one, she had experienced several today, it made her question everything; who she was, if she should be exploring her power, who was watching her as she did so, it was all so terrifying. Her sense of self had been so powerful months ago at the ridge in the east, and now she felt more lost than she was before.

To make matter worse, Dori turned to see her mother congratulating a group of young Meta women she had taken under her wing, expressing how proud she was of them, a statement she had yet to hear today. No matter how much Dori told herself she was okay with her and her mother's relationship it always hurt watching her be more of a mother to others than to her own daughter. The nice moment from this morning faded into the back of her mind and she felt numbness take over her. Dori reminded herself, only a couple months and she would be leaving.

Cyrus appeared next to her and pulled her attention. "Dori," her father said, holding her arms, "I know I've been hard on you this year," he coughed slightly, choking down his pride, not looking directly at her. "And I know I pushed you to do the internship despite your reservations." Cyrus sighed deeply and pulled his focus back to her looking her straight in the face. "I'm glad you had the courage to find your own path, and I'm extremely proud of you,"

Dori's eyes watered, "Thanks, dad."

Cyrus pulled her in for a hug before clearing his throat, "Dinner at Brachya's Buffet right?"

Dori barely got out her excited "Yes", before Cyrus was whisked away for some council photos with the top of the class. Dori gave a small smile as he walked away.

Blythe nearly tackled Dori giving her a noogie and a "Congrats, Doe". After tossing him off her back she smiled at him and gave him a hug. The only member of her family that gave her nothing but joy.

"I told Jareth that some kids were talking about the new vampires policies so he ran to go insert his unwanted opinion on poor freshman," Blythe said beaming with pride.

Dori laughed. "Thanks, that should buy us a little time before dinner," Dori said dreading the dinner ahead. If she were really going to celebrate her graduation she would take Blythe into the island and just have dinner with him and Mae.

Opal and her mom joined the family for a celebratory dinner at Dori's favorite buffet, the only place in the realm that served the leviathan crab. With mounds of fresh buttery Brachyathan in her stomach, Dori snuck away to the east of the island. She had been wanting to see what the Meltembra side of Lithos Ridge looked like after the battle.

Word spread about the beaming lights coming from each stone as the magic gems within them radiated with magnificent flashes during that morning. As Dori approached the ridge, she saw the lights had faded back to a simple glow from each gem, admittedly still brighter than she had seen them prior. The grass was lusher than she had ever seen it and she removed her shoes before finishing her climb to the ridge.

Her sandals dangling from her fingers at her side while the rich grass tickled her feet and the dirt connected her to the earth below, she closed her eyes as she continued to walk reveling in the moment. Approaching the base of the stone circle, she looked and saw the bright gold ring in the middle of stone on the ground, no longer covered in a layer of dust and dirt. Even the specks of magic colors spreading from it to each stone were bright and looked as if they had been polished. The fog cleared from the edge of the ridge and she could see the statue of Queen Dahlia standing still with her arms held out in offering toward the sea. The sparkling of her gold encased hair appeared to be waving in the wind as it glittered in the sunshine.

When Dori heard a voice behind her she turned to see who was there, but saw no one. She looked around and heard the voice even clearer.

"Sweet Endora," the strong deep voice said. "Thank you, for awakening me," his voice said holding the 'me' out enough to make Dori's skin crawl.

Dori was looking in every direction but the voice was all around.

"I'm not done with you yet, darling."

A surge passed over Dori, she saw a brief flash of red sparkles glittering around her and they disappeared with the wind. Left with the lingering feeling of chills, she left the ridge continually looking back over her shoulder. She tried to shake the questions rumbling around in her brain, but that was never something she was very good at. The pangs in her gut returned ever so slightly. She wiggled out all her extremities determined to shake off the bad energy and clear her mind. Flitting into fairy form she began to soar over the island, trying to take her mind off it and enjoy the view of Zalor in celebration.

TO BE CONTINUED...

Acknowledgements

EJ, my number one fan and reason why I work so hard.

April, from the very beginning you supported my idea for this series, from helping me build the lore, to finalizing every little detail. BTAM would not have been what it is without your help and support. You are incredible and I'm honored to have you in my life.

Angelica, the first one to read BTAM, you helped me shape what is printed on these pages and bring the magic to life.

Sebastian, you have been one of the biggest supports in my writing, and on days when completing this book was extremely stressful and overwhelming, you were my rock. You have given me comfort and care when I needed it most, and I don't think I can truly express the difference you have made in my life. Thank you for supporting me, encouraging me to chasing my dreams, and loving every bit of my fairy lifestyle.

Jah-Shea and Nyiesha, from day one you have been my biggest cheerleaders and allowed me to truly embrace my potential. You have helped me recognize a piece of myself that I thought was lost. Endora's story changed because you both changed mine.

Writers Obscurity, my team. By shear happenstance we were pulled together, and there is nothing more magical than what has come from our group. My biggest supporters, you have made me a better writer, and the author I am today is because you helped me get here.

Thank you to all those who encouraged me along the way, this journey was possible because of you.

The circle of supernatural that make up my *found family* are so unique; not belonging to any one faction because they don't fit in a box. They fill life with laughter and love, and I am so grateful they have chosen to share their magic with me.

Thank you all for being an integral part of my world, and helping me bring to life the magic of Meltembra.

More On The Author
Tori Einher

Born and raised in South Jersey, Einher has made it her life's mission to not let her past take over her life. She has been writing since a young age and finally found her true passion for the art in creating the Wings of Alchemy series.

Einher moved away for college, where she earned a BS in Business and Biblical Studies. Since then Einher has lived many places; from a boat on the West Coast to the mountains of North Carolina and the rivers by Niagara Falls. Travel and adventure are embedded deep in her spirit; Einher is always planning the next adventure. Einher returned to school to earn a certificate in Graphic Design, to pursue creating a success business.

When she's not writing, Einher is spending time with her family and friends in Western New York, working on her next design project, traveling, going to concerts, or cosplaying and attending conventions and fairs all over!

"Creating this series gave me the courage to find my wings, and I truly feel like I have never been more authentic than I am today. Creating Endora helped me step into my happily ever after; living a life of confidence, adventure, and magic. Thank you for helping make this dream a reality."

~Tori

Stay Tuned For Book 2

Beyond The Lotus Falls

SCAN FOR MORE
ON TORI AND
UNSCRIPTED CHAOS